The Colour Of Kerosene
And Other Stories

Cameron Raynes

16pt

Read How You Want
LARGE PRINT BOOKS, BRAILLE & DAISY

Copyright Page from the Original Book

Wakefield Press
1 The Parade West
Kent Town
South Australia 5067
www.wakefieldpress.com.au

First published 2012

Cover and illustrations by Robin Green
Designed and typeset by Robin Green
Printed and bound by Hyde Park Press, Adelaide

National Library of Australia Cataloguing-in-Publication entry

Author: Raynes, Cameron, 1964-
Title: The colour of kerosene and other stories / Cameron Raynes.

Dewey Number: A823.4

Government
of South Australia
Arts SA

fox creek
wines

Australian Government

Publication of this book was assisted by
the Commonwealth Government through the
Australia Council, its arts funding and advisory body.

TABLE OF CONTENTS

Wakefield Press

The Colour of Kerosene and Other Stories

Cameron Raynes has worked in Perth, Meekatharra, Katherine, Darwin and Adelaide as a barman, welfare worker, anthropologist, historian, archivist, editor, academic and scriptwriter. He has a PhD on the moral subtext of Aboriginal oral history and writes whenever he can. He lives in Semaphore and is currently writing a script for a feature film based on his story, 'The Colour of Kerosene'.

By the same author

The Last Protector: The illegal removal of Aboriginal children from their parents in South Australia

'A Little Flour and a Few Blankets': An administrative history of Aboriginal Affairs in South Australia, 1834–2000

For Tania

The Colour of Kerosene

It felt wrong from the moment he picked up the fare outside the hotel on Marine Terrace.

'Turn here,' the man said.

They drove on, almost to the end of Rifle Range Road. 'That's the one,' said the man, pointing to a weatherboard, Housing Commission house with a dying wattle out the front.

'Didn't know you could kill them,' said Luke.

The man didn't answer. He hadn't said much since talking Luke into the job, ten minutes earlier. A three-hundred-kilometre trip to the east, to a station. The promise of a six-hundred-dollar fare and a tank of free diesel when he got there. It was too good to pass up. Luke could use the money.

The man wound down his window, leant a meaty arm across Luke and depressed the horn – two, three times. 'Jess!' he shouted.

They waited. The front door opened and a woman appeared. Her dress was shapeless but for the slightest hint of hips as she came down the steps. A still-pretty face, dirty blonde hair, meagre breasts, she had the same unnaturally translucent blue eyes as the man.

'Where's Annabel?' asked the man.

'Inside. She's coming.' Jess stood beside his door, passing a Coke bag from hand to hand. 'Pete. Are you sure I should come?'

'Get in,' he said, nodding towards the back seat.

She opened the back door and climbed in.

*

Annabel looked a couple of years older than Jess, in her late twenties perhaps. Smooth, brown skin, and lots of it. They headed east, the nude hills of the Geraldton plains, stripped of their trees a century before, leaning into them on both sides as the car climbed into the marginal country. Behind him, Luke heard the gurgle of fluid sluicing out of a bladder and into a cup, smelt the sweet stink of cheap wine. It occurred to him that it was not too late to turn back.

'Jess, you get to meet the Greek,' said Pete.

Annabel laughed – a gurgling, resonant chuckle. For Luke, it was hard to hear that laugh and not think of her body and how it must look, feel, smell.

*

Fifty minutes later, approaching Mullewa, Pete leant over, his breath sour and hot on Luke's face.

'How's ya fuel?'

Luke looked at the gauge. 'About a third,' he said. 'Should I get some here?'

'Nah. We'll make it. Two hundred clicks to go. You can fill up there. Take all ya want.'

The Railway Hotel on their left, worn out rolling stock on their right, a church, dusty roads lined with ugly cottages, their yards defeated by drought, a petrol station. Not a soul in sight. By the time they'd reached the '80' sign on the outskirts of town, Luke was doing a hundred and ten.

Pete fiddled with the glove box and opened it. Luke turned to him as a road train blasted past on his right and tried to make a point of holding his gaze.

'Hey! What's this?' said Pete, rummaging among Luke's rego papers and petrol receipts. 'Didn't know you were packin' heat.' He laughed, holding the little blue water pistol that Luke's nephew had left there the week before.

'Put it back,' said Luke.

'Spray me,' said Annabel, gurgling. A sound like water going to waste.

'I'll piss in it at the next stop,' said Pete. He rested his hand on the dash, pointing the pistol at a LandCruiser rushing towards them. His arms were brown, scarred, his forearms as thick as pythons. Not the defined, neat muscles of the gym, they were arms you got from working outside, straining fences, hoisting bales of hay, holding an animal still while someone else worked on its horns, teeth, or balls.

We're not stopping, thought Luke, eyes on the odometer, willing it to tick over, conscious of the needle on the fuel gauge falling backwards.

*

An hour later, the car full of cigarette smoke, he pulled up at a truck stop. Pete belched, opened his door and got out. He stood in front of the car, his back to them, pissing. Luke resisted the temptation to throw the car into reverse and roar away. They were now closer to the station than to Mullewa, and he wasn't sure his fuel would last. *Maybe if the car was empty of passengers...*

Luke turned to look at the girls.

'Anyone else?' he asked.

Annabel ignored him. Luke looked out the passenger-side window. Flat land all around, the car hemmed in by scrubby bushland as if the world ended at fifty paces in each direction. Pete had stopped pissing and was throwing rocks at the 'Rest area' sign, thirty metres away. Jess groaned.

'You okay?' Luke asked.

She shook her head, fumbled with the handle, opened the door, leant out and vomited loudly onto the ground. Luke popped the boot and got out.

'She's always been like that,' Pete said, aiming at the sign. 'Since she was a kid.' The sound of rock hitting metal and he shouted, triumphant.

Luke got a container of water from the boot and poured some into Jess's cupped hands. She spat, then brought her hands up to her face, rinsed, then spat again.

*

'Not far now,' said Pete.

Ahead, the road veered to the left. The day was easing into dusk and the scrub racing by was softened by shadows, its upper foliage picked out here and there in gold.

A 44-gallon drum marked the turn-off to the station. Luke concentrated, keeping his wheels out of the deep ruts that scored the track. It looked like it hadn't been graded for years.

Through one open gate, then another, then past a row of dark, misshapen pines, their lower limbs hacked away. Then a homestead squatting in the gloom, its veranda sagging. He opened the windows to the smell of pine and wood smoke. The needle on the fuel gauge didn't even move when he turned off the engine.

The Greek was skinny, with a beer belly. Late forties, face and nose reddened by booze and sun. He emerged from the side of the homestead. The girls and Pete got out. Luke stayed where he was, keys in the ignition. Pete said something to the Greek, and he spoke back, too soft for Luke to hear.

Pete came round to Luke's side of the car and leant on it.

'Pump's locked.'

'Locked?'

'Yeah. We're gonna have to wait for Frank.'

'Who the fuck is Frank?' said Luke, fighting to keep the thin vein of panic rising in his body from coming out his mouth.

'Manager. Got the key. Should be back in a coupla hours.'

'A couple of hours!?'

'Gonna have to wait. He's got your money too.'

*

The five of them sat on the veranda, cards in hand, the light from a pair of battered hurricane lamps spilling around and leaking into the night.

The Greek was organised. He had a box of casino chips – everything from ones to fifties – a brand new pack of cards, a slab of beer beside him. Luke hadn't wanted to play.

'Might as well,' suggested Pete. 'Fuck all else to do.'

Luke cashed in the twenty-five dollars he had left in his wallet and took his first hand of poker. Jacks and threes and he won fifteen dollars with the Greek seeing him with a pair of kings. Luke soon had a hundred dollars in chips in front of him and he relaxed a little and took the beer that the Greek offered. The girls stopped playing.

'Jess,' said Pete, nodding his head towards the front door. 'Get us somethin' to eat will ya?'

She shuffled off and came back a minute later with a bowl of beer nuts and a bowl of chips. The game changed to blackjack and somewhere around his third beer, Luke realised he wouldn't be driving anywhere that night, even if

Frank turned up. He sighed, nodding gently to himself, a jack and a nine on the floorboards in front of him. He had twenty-five dollars riding on it, Pete had bust, and the Greek, the banker, had a queen and a seven.

'Might as well go for it,' said Pete, and the Greek smiled and his red face glowed and he turned over the three of clubs.

That was the start of a bad run for Luke. By the time he'd finished his fifth beer, Annabel was writing down his borrowings. She did it on Jess's calf, with a biro. By midnight, there was a '50' with a line through it, a '100' above it with the same treatment, and above that a '150'.

'That's it,' said Luke, swaying as he got up. 'That's a hundred and fifty I haven't got. I'm goin' to bed.'

In the weird, piney darkness he got the picnic blanket from the boot and climbed into his car. He put the little blue gun carefully back in the glove box, thinking of his sister, Claudia, and their plan, long shelved, to run a bookshop in Geraldton. Thirty-odd-thousand people and no proper bookshop. Maybe there was a reason for that. He laughed. He made sure each door was locked, then reclined his seat and draped the blanket over his chest.

At one point he woke up, hearing someone shout. He wound down his window a notch, heard Jess's voice, pleading, 'I couldn't do nothin' about it.' He wound the window back up.

He was the first one up. He went for a walk, past the pines and towards a small rise to the west. Stunted eucalypts all around him and as far as he could see. A busted-up fence in front of him, the wires all brown and broken and tangled. *Tetanus,* he thought. There wasn't an animal in sight.

It brought back a memory of one of his family's more disastrous 'holidays'. He'd been about ten. His dad had camped them beside a murky, mosquito-infested waterhole and had spent three days crisscrossing the ground with a hired metal detector, searching for gold, finding nothing but the bottle tops and ring-pulls left by the fossickers before them. On the fourth morning, on seeing her third 'holiday snake', as his father called them, Luke's mum had shut them all up in the car and tooted the horn until her husband, grubby with dirt and frustration, had relented and packed up his gear.

Walking back to the homestead, Luke found the diesel pump near the first gate, behind a water tank. The padlock's shackle was as thick as his finger. There were a couple of fist-size rocks dumped beside the tank. He picked one up and kept walking.

Jess was on the veranda, her head sticking out of a bundle of blankets. Her face tried a smile, gave up and fell back on itself. He walked up to her and stood in front of the veranda. Her eyes were the colour of kerosene. He couldn't hold her stare.

'Is Frank back yet?'

Jess shook her head. Luke remembered he was holding a rock and moved his arm behind his hip.

'What's going on here?' he asked.

'Whatdaya mean?' she said, softly.

Luke gestured with a nod of his head towards the west. 'Where's the animals? I thought this was sheep country.'

Jess frowned. 'Dunno. Never been here before. I dunno why anyone would want to live out here. It's horrible.'

'We came out this way once,' said Luke. 'When I was a kid. Family holiday. Mulga, mallee. Fuck, I don't even know what it's called. I remember saying to my dad, "Why are all the trees so small? Where are all the old trees?"'

'We never had no holidays.'

Luke gave a laugh that died quickly in the back of his throat when he saw she wasn't joking. He let the rock drop with a soft thud behind him. They both pretended not to hear the sound it made.

*

Later, the men came out with plates of bacon and sausage. Jess cooked some for Luke and he sat there with them.

'He'll be here soon,' said Pete.

Luke said nothing, ate everything on his plate and then put it down beside him on the veranda. He watched as the

Greek got the cards out again, cut them, shuffled and placed two cards in front of him, picture-side up.

'Double or nuttin'?' asked the Greek. Luke knew this game: In-Betweens, or Stupid, as it was sometimes called.

It was one of the simplest games.

'Okay,' said Luke.

It was a generous offer. He had a king and a four in front of him and had just been offered double or nothing on a hundred and fifty dollars that the next card the Greek turned up would land between them.

The Greek turned over the four of hearts and shook his head. 'Your luck will change,' he said, dealing him another two cards. This hand was even better. A king and a two. Luke looked at him.

'Okay,' said the Greek. 'Hey, we like you. You're a good boy. Same as last time? Double or nuttin'?

Anything other than an ace, a two, or a king and his debt would dissolve and they'd still owe him the six-hundred-dollar fare. Luke nodded. When the Greek turned over the two of spades it was like everything in his life had been building towards that one moment in time and he just kept nodding.

'Looks like we're just about square,' said the Greek. He wouldn't look at Luke, and Luke could see Pete out of the corner of his eye, grinning. Annabel stifled a laugh. Luke got up from the veranda and walked over to his car and then just stood there, leaning against the driver's door.

*

In the late afternoon, sitting in his car, he felt something drop into his lap. He looked up. Jess's dirty blonde hair and tired face over his right shoulder.

'I'm coming with you,' she said.

He looked down. There was a key in his lap.

'I seen them both go out the back, down to the dump. I dunno what they're doin'.'

Luke sat there. He had the vague feeling that he was being set up.

'I seen them go,' said Jess, her voice urgent and coarse.

They pushed the car over to the pump. Jess filled it as Luke sat in the driver's seat, fingering his keys. She jumped in next to him. The car exploded into life and Luke gunned it, dust pouring out behind. He pointed it at the track, nearly hit the gate, and then they were through.

'Those boys are screwed up,' said Jess when they were clear of the station. 'Didn't let me sleep hardly at all last night.'

'Who's with who?' asked Luke.

Jess shrugged. 'Doesn't matter. Pete says for men it's like lancing a boil or somefink,' she said. She moved in her seat, adjusting her skirt. 'Says you gotta get the poison out before it drives ya crazy. Says he's gotta do it every day.'

Luke looked at her legs, looked back at the track.

'He'd probly do it with the Greek,' Jess said. 'If there was no one else around.'

'He's your brother?'

'Step,' she said. 'Same mum. Different dad. But mine didn't hang around either. Mum never had no luck wiv men.'

'Where's Frank?' Luke asked as they turned onto the main highway.

'Frank's dead.'

Luke nodded, humming a tune to the sound of the wind rushing by. She started telling him how she'd been abused by her stepfather, a fisherman her mother had taken up with after her own father had wandered off.

'I'm sorry,' said Luke. 'I don't want to hear that.'

'Saved your life,' she said. 'You owe me.'

She stretched out her hand and it touched his thigh lightly, then settled on the handbrake. Her left leg was turned to him, resting on her right knee. He could see the '50', the '100' and the '150' of his debt written on her leg. His mother's 'holiday snakes' suddenly came to mind and he laughed out loud.

The low, ugly trees whipped by the window. Luke knew he'd have to stop the car soon, relieve himself. Where he was headed was endless glare and haze. The road curved and then straightened out, lancing the sun.

Granite Country

It was still dark when we set off from Albany. Despite the sleeping pills, Catherine had woken around five am. Soon after, when the coffee pot crashed to the kitchen floor, I was awake as well.

We headed north, from where the bad news had come. Three hours later we were on the Forrest Highway, barrelling past Mandurah, nothing but sand beneath the road, nothing but blue sky above. Everything I looked at had a Ken Done feel to it. Hard lines, bright shapes, cartoon colours. I couldn't help thinking what a selfish bastard Scott was.

*

Uncle Gary seemed to have things in hand. Fat, decked out in gold jewellery and a well-meaning smile, he was in touch with the coroner, the police, the undertaker. No one likes a suicide.

'Leave it all to me,' he said, fingers clasped, chunky gold rings glinting as we sat at Gino's, an outdoor cafe in Fremantle, watching the locals. They were all a lot more colourful than the people we knew back home.

'Thanks,' said Catherine, her hand clutching mine underneath the table.

'At least he waited for your mother to die,' said Uncle Gary, and Catherine's nails bit into my palm and I winced with pain. Uncle Gary mistook it for distaste and started to apologise, not to Catherine but to me. We left soon after, amicably enough, Catherine's macaroon untouched on the plate, and when I looked over my shoulder Uncle Gary was raising it to his mouth, watching us as we went.

*

We stayed that night, and the next, with Catherine's mad, lovely Aunty Dot, in a beautiful old weatherboard house in Cottesloe that reminded us both of our own home in Albany. We drank wine with her and ate Coq a Vin from a recipe she'd brought back from France thirty years ago at the end of her bohemian sojourn. Around midnight, we both took pills to help us sleep.

We woke to the smell of ocean and pine trees and sunlight streaming into our room and I pulled her slight body close and she opened up to me and we rocked back and forth very slowly, very gently, aware of a squeak in the innards of the bed, until both of us were done.

Aunty Dot had left beach towels out for us the night before so we walked to the end of her street, across the road and onto the beach. The sand was clean and white and much finer than it was at home and the water not as cold. We swam out past the Cottesloe buoy and floated on our backs, side by side, talking rubbish to each other and to the gulls as the diazepam wore off.

*

Later that morning, we went to the house Scott had been sharing with two fellow architects on the Swan River, near Claremont. Though it was rundown, with cracks in the walls and a trough for a laundry, it had a great view of the river and must have cost a fortune to rent.

Inside, the walls were covered with art, some of it Scott's. There were too many pastels for my liking, though his latest, still on the easel, had great blocks of textured oil and even the bright colours had a dirtiness to them that suggested Albany and the paintings of Guy Grey-Smith.

'He always said you had to travel north if you wanted to make it,' said Catherine as I surveyed his room, noting the absence of photos, stepping around piles of crumpled clothes. 'To be where the action is,' she added. I knew all about this. Scott had referred to both of us, more than once, as 'moss on granite'. She was looking for something and it felt like I was intruding so I left her in his room and walked out to the back of the house.

The backyard was a wasteland of sand. One of Scott's housemates was sitting at a plastic table, smoking. He picked up his pack of Winnie blues and held them out to me but I shook my head. He saw me taking in the shambolic backyard.

'We're just renting,' he said. 'Couldn't afford to buy anything around here if we saved for a thousand years.'

*

There was a surprisingly large turnout for Scott's funeral. Uncle Gary was happy to take the credit for that and moved among the guests like a hot-dog vendor at the footy. Pressing the flesh, generous with homilies and kind words. We stood in the shade of a lemon-scented gum as the funeral director spoke about Scott's love of the outdoors, of art and how it was impossible to take the country out of the boy.

Catherine dropped a postcard she'd found in his room into the open grave. Dog Rock, the dog shaped rock in the heart of Albany. His favourite rock in the world when he was a kid, when he still wanted to be a geologist.

Scott had visited us in Albany once or twice, checking to see if Catherine was looking after his share of the inheritance – the little weatherboard cottage we thought of as home. Over beers he'd talked about the houses he designed.

'Terrible things,' he told me. 'No eaves. No verandas. Feature garages.'

I laughed at that.

'Every time you park your car you gas the kids with carbon monoxide. Only the poor people buy them.'

After the service, we drove back through the river-viewed parts of Nedlands, Claremont and Peppermint Grove, awed and appalled by the wealth. Albany's old, tired money – its shabby gentility, its stone houses with whitewashed walls scoured by wind – was nothing compared to this.

*

Around three am that night, when the drugs and the wine had again lost their battle with my mind, I went to the kitchen for a glass of water. Aunty Dot was at the kitchen table, wrapped in a dressing gown, a tumbler of whisky at her side, playing patience.

'Can't sleep?' she asked.

'No.'

She gathered in the cards and shuffled them expertly. 'Fancy a game?'

'Sure,' I said, sitting down opposite her.

'Strip poker?'

I laughed out loud.

*

When I went back to Catherine there was a bowlful of moonlight spilt on the bed and I thought some of God's carelessness is beautiful but I knew that 'carelessness' was really too kind and that He was just utterly indifferent. But we were returning today, to our little cottage clinging to the side of Mt Clarence, the wind straight off the Southern Ocean, ceaselessly trying to fling us northward. But we wouldn't shift. There was nothing for us here.

I stood in the doorway. Catherine was curled up, fast asleep, her hair dark against her pale face, the shadows in the folds of the doona like tiny ravines and gullies scoring a miniature mountain range. The image of Aunty Dot coyly removing the gown from her shoulders – perhaps her last mad bohemian flourish – to reveal two pendulous, milky-white breasts, flitted across my mind, but I was comforted by the thought that soon we'd be gone from this sandy place, back to the granite country, the south, the eons-dense rock beneath our feet.

Sunlight

For three days straight, Anna had stayed inside, limbs aching, senses dulled. She heard Tom come and go – mainly go. She lay on the bed, watching the fan spin slowly above her. The fever had gone. She felt drained but light. Hungry. Downstairs, in the kitchen, she made herself toast and coffee.

It was Saturday. She had a ten am appointment. Harry. On the table in front of her sat a jar of lemons, packed in salt.

*

Tom wasn't sure why he'd followed Anna to Fremantle. They'd met in Kalgoorlie and lived there in an old miner's cottage on a wide street one back from the row of gaudy, corrugated-iron brothels in Hay Street. It was a fine life – endless, disused tracks to explore by car, frosty winter mornings, an earthy rawness you couldn't find on the coast. Tom had never told her about his vasectomy. He'd had it done before he knew her.

He'd agreed with her that children were a blessing, had been attentive in the bedroom, had encouraged her to become an art therapist. He had done what he could.

*

With her notebook and art gear arranged beside her on the upstairs balcony, waiting for Harry, Anna thought again of a conversation she'd had with Tom before she fell ill.

Tom had come home late from work. Harry's drawings were on the kitchen table. When she walked into the kitchen she saw Tom, stubbie in hand, looking at one of them. It was a picture of Harry flying above the rooftops of the houses on the hillside below their balcony window.

'It's good, isn't it?' said Anna.

'For an autistic kid, I guess.'

Anna hesitated.

'What would be the magic power you'd most like to have?' she asked.

Tom flinched and came out of his dreaminess, defensive.

'To be invisible,' he said at last, keeping his eyes on the picture.

'All the time?' Anna asked.

'No.' He looked at her. 'I mean, to be able to turn invisible when I want to.'

'Why?'

'Fuck! What is this?' Tom slammed his stubbie onto the kitchen table, making Anna jump. 'I need some space,' he said, walking out of the room.

*

Harry kneeled on the veranda, a sheet of paper on the easel in front of him, a row of watercolour pencils in a neat rainbow at his side. He loved this place, this upstairs veranda perched high on the hill overlooking Fremantle.

'That's good,' said Anna, looking over his shoulder.

Harry ignored her, crushing blue pigment under his finger to make sky. Anna took a sip of water and looked at Harry. Thin legs, small-boy shorts, black curls against a bright red T-shirt. She knew she should be trying to engage him, to find new ways to bring him out of himself. But this was clearly what he loved. Sitting above the world, drawing himself into it. Always the same picture.

She sat cross-legged on the veranda, breathing in the jasmine entwining its rails. And she had made real progress. Months had passed since she'd had to hold Harry to her, rubbing his back and his thin shoulders as a tantrum subsided.

The alarm clock beside her rang. Harry put his hands over his ears until Anna turned it off. He started to pack away the crayons, placing each in its rainbow order. Anna pointed to the picture he'd just drawn, to his hair swept back by the air rushing past him as he flew.

'I love that,' she said.

'That shows you're moving,' said Harry, carefully not looking at her.

*

Tom pulled out into the traffic on Stirling Highway, glad to be on his way home. He hated doing house maintenance – even more for the eighteen dollars an hour it gave him. At times he felt as if he was the only person in Western Australia earning less than a hundred thousand a year. Living in Fremantle, earning this sort of money. It couldn't last. In six months he'd gone through most of his savings, and knew it was probably the same for Anna. In another six months he'd be in debt. He thought of going back to Kal, working on the mines for a year or two. He'd come back and put down a deposit on a simple two-bedroom house, as close to Freo as money would allow. The car in front slowed then turned left without indicating and he gave it a long blast with his horn.

*

Anna poured herself another coffee and took it out to their tiny backyard, separated from the others like it on both sides by an untidy brush fence. The young mother next door had laid on morning tea for her playgroup. Anna sat down, waiting for Tom to come home. She could hear the hungry squawking of a newborn, chatter from the new mothers.

'Sunlight is a natural disinfectant,' she heard someone say, and she thought of the lemons on the kitchen table. She felt good, strong. The sickness nearly gone from her body, she felt on the verge of being well, and the feeling was somehow better than wellness itself.

*

Anna lay on her side in bed, watching Tom as he placed a glass of water on his bedside table and climbed in beside her.

'It was Harry's last day today,' said Anna. 'They're moving to Victoria.'

Tom lay on his back, staring at the ceiling.

Anna hesitated. 'I wonder how we'd cope with a son like Harry,' she said.

'We wouldn't.'

'You just have to, don't you?' said Anna, surprised by Tom's response.

'I wouldn't cope. I'd be at the pub.'

Tom rolled away from Anna, towards the wall.

'You can talk to me, you know.'

Tom closed his eyes.

*

Anna sat at the table, dressed simply, but with her hair tied up. The table was set for two, complete with champagne and flutes. She checked her phone and dialled a number. Tom's voice answered. 'Tom's phone. Leave a message and I'll get back to you.'

She put the phone down and rummaged through the papers on the kitchen bench. She found Harry's painting and stuck it on the fridge with masking tape. Later, in bed, Anna was woken by a noise downstairs. She sat up and heard the rustling of papers and then footsteps in the hallway and then the front door opening and closing. She lay back down and closed her eyes.

*

In the morning, still dressed in her pyjamas, the first thing she saw when she entered the kitchen was Harry's drawing, screwed up and left on the table beside a half-empty stubbie. The sun was just above the horizon, shining through the kitchen window.

Anna went back upstairs and began stuffing clothes into her backpack. In the kitchen she unscrunched Harry's painting, rolled it up and stashed it with her clothes. She squeezed the jar of preserved lemons in, turned, and walked out of the room.

On the doorstep, she hesitated. Below her was the crazy, cramped roofscape of Fremantle. An image of Tom, in bed, rolling away from her, filled her mind and she started walking, the first rays of sunlight on her face, the breeze off the ocean making streamers of her hair.

Semaphore

I had no intention of killing anything. In my defence, I had not slept for twenty-four hours and was unhinged. As you would be, given what happened last night. But no more on that. It doesn't reflect well on me.

After breakfast, Sarah put her arm around me. She asked if I could do her a favour, and of course I said 'Yes'. I am, after all, her brother-in-law.

She had an assignment to deliver – the last essay for her social work degree.

'Absolutely,' I said. 'Leave them to me. We'll take a walk down to the beach. We'll have fun, won't we girls?'

Her two girls nodded dutifully, clearly dubious. But when I mentioned ice-creams, their spirits lifted. They were six and eight.

As she got ready to go to uni, I listened half-heartedly to some wank on Radio National about the amorality of tourists and their lack of obligation to anything but their own enjoyment and experience.

We waved goodbye to Sarah on her way to town. Her house was in Semaphore, five untidy streets back from the seaweedy pond they call the ocean. On my arrival the previous day, I had immediately felt at a disadvantage. Unfamiliar territory. I was surprised by the general shabbiness of things. It seemed that the poor lived by the water, as if the Sydney dictum of banishing the unwashed and needy to the west had been transplanted to Adelaide, regardless of the fact that the sun sets over water here. Perhaps Adelaideans think living by the ocean is vulgar.

*

Sarah had organised the girls' bathers, towels, food and water. They made it clear that I was their pack mule. I acquiesced in this, unclear about where I should draw the line, or what the line even looked like. I'm not used to children — not even my brother's. Todd shouldn't have left Sarah like he did. He shouldn't have gone off with a woman ten years younger than her and put me in this situation, with choices to make and regret.

The beachfront was a short stroll away, past a row of unkempt flats and a low-roofed boarding house. All the tables were taken at the little cafe on the esplanade, full of women in tracksuits and big sunglasses, keeping watch over their Caitlins, Jaydyns, Zacs and Jacks, playing on the boat-shaped playground. I let the girls play there until they got bored, then we walked down to the beach.

*

From the moment I saw the dog I knew there was going to be trouble. It was the way it loped past the seagulls, not bothering to chase them. Of course, the type (bull terrier) and the accessory (studded collar) did nothing to help, or the fact that the person holding the leash, to which of course the dog was not attached, was perhaps thirteen, with a rat-tail and a sour look to match.

The dog kept slouching towards the girls, and I raised myself from my towel. Emily, the eight-year-old, saw the dog and stopped digging. I called out to them as it closed in. They looked blankly at me as I ran at them. Fiona put her hand out to pat the dog and it snapped, grabbing her hand and dropping its front legs. She screamed. The boy was there now, hitting his dog on the head with the fleshy, bottom part of his fist. I didn't bother with subtleties. As I reached the group at a full run, I jumped feet first into the dog. It grunted, releasing its grip on Fiona.

'You bastard,' yelled Rat-tail. I rolled over and got to my knees as the dog leapt at my face. I just managed to knock it slightly off course with a forearm and grabbed a handful of fur near its neck. I lifted it off its feet and fell on it, my elbow wedged behind its jaw.

'Get off him!'

'Piss off,' I said. I felt his fist land on my head and I swung around with my free elbow and collected him in the face. He screamed.

At that point I was stuck. I couldn't let the dog go: it would bite me or one of the girls. There was nothing else to be done. I slipped a hand under the dog's collar and hoisted it over my shoulder. The dog grunted and struggled, strangling beneath its own weight. The kid was still lying on the beach, holding his face and crying.

I strode out towards the horizon. An elderly man in red Speedos watched me as I went. A young man fishing from the jetty stopped reeling in his line. The gulf bed angled gently downward, and it wasn't until perhaps sixty metres from the shore that I was in deep-enough water. I didn't look around. I knew everyone would be watching.

The dog was still struggling. It was weakened by now and it was a very simple matter to roll it over my shoulder and into the water. I kept a tight grip on its collar and its head underwater. It was surprisingly simple to drown. The boy was wading out to where I was, tears streaming down his face. By the time he got out to me, I could let the dog go. I pushed it gently at him, as you would a toy boat, and walked back to the shore.

*

Rat-tail followed us home, carrying his dripping, dead dog, swearing at me the whole way. On the doorstep I turned to him.

'You'd better go now. I'm sorry about your dog. You should've had him on a lead.'

His face was flushed from the effort of carrying the dog.

'You're fucked mister, fucked in the head.'

'Just keep going,' I said, motioning with my hand.

'I'm going to bring my father over. He'll fuckin' kill you.'

'Well it's not my house. I don't live here.'

'Where do you live then?'

'Nowhere.' And I slammed shut the door and let the sound of two girls' gentle sobbing wash over me.

*

The Wind and the Salt

By the time they arrived at the caravan park, Martin hadn't spoken to his son for an hour. A sea breeze whipped across the camping ground. Daniel, still silent, was pressed by his father to help with the tent. Rachel busied herself emptying gear from the boot of the car. At a critical point the wind gusted and Daniel dropped the pole he was holding. The tent sagged and Martin swore as Daniel looked on, his fourteen-year-old face void of expression. For Martin, the squeal of the wind in the casuarinas bordering their site was almost as bad as the closed-up silence of the car.

The five-hour drive from Adelaide to Yorke Peninsula had taken them through Martin's hometown and he had felt an urge to visit his old school to see if the tree he'd planted was still there. Maybe on the way back.

*

Sally and Gordon arrived on the edge of dusk. Martin helped them set up tent and then the three of them retreated to the communal kitchen where Rachel was cooking dinner. Over beers, steak and sausages at a slatted wooden table, they planned the next few days. Gordon was keen to try out his new rod and Martin was willing to tag along and 'wet a line'. Rachel and Sally wanted to look at some local real estate.

His meal finished, Daniel dug his iPod out of his backpack and began playing a game.

'What about you, Daniel?' asked Gordon. 'Coming fishing with us tomorrow?'

Daniel looked up quickly from the screen and stole a glance at his mother. Rachel said nothing. Daniel grimaced. 'If I have to,' he said. He didn't look at Martin.

*

Martin stood alongside Sally, wiping the dishes as she washed and stacked. It was two years since Martin had found her on Facebook and sent her the message that had rekindled their high-school friendship. But this was their first shared holiday.

Sally and Gordon had lost their only child, Kate, five years ago. Martin had the feeling they had locked the world out for much of the first few years and had grown away from some of their friends. Kate would have been a year older than Daniel.

When the dishes were done and the leftovers Glad-wrapped and stowed away, Martin kissed Sally on the cheek, said goodnight, and walked back to his tent. It was the first time he'd kissed her since high school.

*

Martin slept lightly until an hour or so before dawn and then lay there, not wanting to get the day off to a bad start by stumbling around a campsite in the dark. He thought of work, then of Flanagan, his bow-tie-wearing colleague in the Department of Environmental Science. Older, louder, and with flamboyance to burn, Flanagan had been a climate-change denier in the early 2000s, his research stumped up by oil interests.

Flanagan's three children were in their mid to late thirties and were all, if Flanagan could be believed, near the top of their professions. He put it down to having brought them up on a half-acre block in the hills, with nature on their doorstep. At a faculty meeting he showed photos of his renovated bluestone cottage. All the women sighed and the men stared for a second then passed them on and muttered about 'oil money' later, in the linoleumed corridor.

*

At breakfast, Daniel toyed with his cereal, his iPod on, playing a game. Martin tried to fire him up with the idea of catching fish for dinner. The beach was several kilometres away, on the southern side of the point. Daniel grunted and kept his eyes on the screen.

'Alright,' said Martin. 'I think you need a break from that thing.'

Daniel ignored him and took another spoonful of Weet-Bix. This was his punishment, Martin knew, for being so selfish as to deny Daniel a sibling.

'Hand it over,' said Martin. 'It's holiday time.'

Daniel looked across the table at his mother. Rachel shrugged her shoulders. Gordon, sitting alongside her, carefully studied the fishing guide he'd got from the van park store.

'Fine,' snapped Daniel, pushing the iPod away. He got up, went to the kitchen bench and returned with another Weet-Bix in his bowl, frosted with a thick layer of sugar.

When he'd finished it he got up, went to the bench, put another biscuit in his bowl and sat down again. Gordon was showing Martin the rig he used to catch whiting. Martin glanced up and Daniel gave him his flat look. Rachel excused herself and left.

When Daniel went to the kitchen bench for his fifth helping of Weet-Bix, Martin exploded, banging his fist on the slatted table. Gordon put his hand on Martin's shoulder. 'It's alright,' he said. 'Let me handle it. Go get your gear ready.'

At their campsite, Rachel was organising towels and snorkelling gear for their trip to the beach. She had Daniel's surfboard out. They had bought it for his birthday, five months ago, and it had stood in the corner of his room since then, collecting dust. Martin told her what had happened.

'Maybe he thinks you only ever *take* things from him,' she said.

'Oh, so you're on his side, are you?'

Rachel rolled her eyes. 'No,' she said. 'I just think that maybe you need to offer some incentives. Ticks *and* crosses.'

'It's gone way beyond that,' said Martin. She didn't get it, he knew. She didn't see the political nuances that surrounded every interaction he had with his son. 'We've moved into new territory,' he added. She crossed her arms and turned side-on to him.

'It's a war,' he said.

'Well, it's a war you can't win.'

'Then we'll just both have to lose,' said Martin. Even as he said it he knew what a terrible thing it was to say and he could see the seamless corridor and Flanagan's smug face.

*

They returned from their fishing trip with half a dozen bony whiting. Later, Martin drove his family north, through the dullest landscape he could imagine, relieved only by a string of drab towns with boarded up shops and buildings no taller than lemon trees. The Barkers hung on their tail, a hundred metres behind them in their Corolla.

'When can I have my iPod back?' asked Daniel.

'When I can see you're making an effort–' began Martin, struggling to work out what to say next. He realised he couldn't remember the last time Daniel had smiled at him. He scanned the road ahead for kangaroos.

'An effort?' asked Daniel.

'Well, yes. When I can see you're taking an interest in something that doesn't involve electrical circuits and a screen.'

'Like?'

'Like the world around you, for instance.'

Daniel stared out at the flatness rushing past.

The thing that had really pissed Martin off was what Flanagan had written on the 'Ideas' board in the staffroom: 'The failures of our children speak to us in a clear, merciless way, of our own developmental failures'. Martin had no answer for that. At one point he'd rubbed it off, only to find it up again two days later. Then someone else had rubbed it off, for good.

*

Martin stopped outside the Your Property shop in Edithburgh. Two pubs, a post office, half a dozen tacky shops. Daniel got out 'to stretch my legs in the outside world' as he put it and began walking towards the ocean. The four adults climbed up onto the veranda of the real estate office to look at the properties displayed in the window. Martin beckoned Rachel over to a photo of a run-down homestead on one acre between Edithburgh and Yorketown. 'Yuck,' said Rachel. 'You'd have to fight off the snakes.' She slid off sideways to see what Sally was ooo-ing about.

Martin turned around to see his son a hundred metres away, at the edge of the sea cliff, holding onto the railing. Daniel looked skinny, his windcheater loose and flapping around him in the breeze.

'Whatya thinking?' asked Gordon.

'The mortgage,' said Martin. Two-hundred-and-seventy-five thousand in the red after the renos, at nearly eight percent, and the interest alone bleeding close to two grand each month.

'Making any headway?' asked Gordon. The old checked shirt he wore was flecked with blood.

'Nup. You?'

'Nup.'

Sally and Rachel came out of the shop with the real estate agent in tow. A thin man with a smile that came and went. Martin had to look at him twice to convince himself he wasn't the tight-faced kid who'd been ostracised at his school, twenty-odd years ago. What was his name? This man's name was Craig and that didn't ring any bells for Martin.

Craig let them into a two-storey town house with sweeping views of the back of the pub and occasional glimpses of ocean. Rachel and Sally weaved through the rooms, taking careful note of built-in storage space while Martin, Gordon and Daniel tagged along behind them, getting stuck in doorways.

*

Back at the van park, in the communal kitchen, Martin tried to read a book that a colleague had recommended, on the social construction of knowledge. The words buzzed and swarmed at him. He put the book down and shut his eyes.

'Fancy a walk?' Sally was standing beside him in a long dress, her hair tied up in a neat bun.

'Sure,' said Martin.

At the edge of the park they found a dirt road that branched off towards the dunes. There were sugar gums here and an understorey of native shrubs. Sally looked pretty with her hair up. The sun was getting low and the light slanted in golden and forgiving.

'You wouldn't really move back out this way, would you?' asked Martin.

Sally laughed. 'God no. Can't think of anything worse.'

'Ditto,' said Martin. Ahead, he could see the low sand dunes where the tidal flats began. There was a faint smell of seaweed on the air.

'You remember that kid we all ostracised?' he asked.

Sally stopped walking and turned to him. 'Yeah, I was thinking about him today. That's weird.'

'The real estate agent,' said Martin. 'He looks just like him.'

'Yeah, that's it.' Sally started walking again. 'Charlie,' she added. They were close to the dunes now.

'Charlie,' agreed Martin. 'I'd forgotten his name.' And now that he could name him, a memory came back. He was on his way home from school, watching as the son of the leader of the local bikie gang punched Charlie in the guts and upended his school bag onto the dirt. Martin had stood there, frozen, wishing he was elsewhere.

'I wonder what happened to him,' said Sally, climbing the first dune. Martin followed her, the wind in his face, looking out over the tidal flats to the south where gulls were hunting small creatures in the mud and the shallows. He hoped Charlie was somewhere good, living well, but he couldn't imagine it. He waited until the wind had dried his eyes before he talked again.

*

The property was in the main street of Edithburgh, just a few doors down from the real estate office. They'd decided at breakfast to look at one more house and then round off the day with a visit to the rocky bay so Daniel could try out his board.

Martin and Gordon hung back, on the footpath, eyeing the bakery across the road. Several families were camped at the tables outside, eating pies and pasties. An old man shuffled out from behind the fly-strapped doorway.

Martin saw the old man hesitate as he came to the edge of the pavement. He put his foot out over the road, lowered it too fast and Martin winced out loud as he saw his ankle buckle beneath him and then the old man was down, on the bitumen, groaning.

Martin and Gordon rushed across the road. They helped him up and onto one of the plastic chairs on the pavement. The old man was disoriented and panicky but knew his name was Harold and that he lived around the corner somewhere. He had a sprained ankle and a nasty graze that had peeled away the thin skin of his shin. Martin shivered when he saw it. He held a serviette to Harold's leg to quell the bleeding while Gordon went inside the bakery to see who they should call.

When Craig ambled over with Rachel, Sally and Daniel, Martin asked him if he knew where the old man lived and Craig scratched his head and said, 'Dunno. Must be new to town', and seemed prepared to leave it at that. He checked his watch and then he was gone.

Gordon came out of the bakery, shrugging his shoulders. The staff had suggested they drive him to the health clinic, down the road. Rachel and Sally helped Harold to Martin's car and eased him into the back seat. Daniel jumped in and helped strap him in and Martin smiled at his son and said, 'Thanks, mate.'

But the bakery staff hadn't mentioned that the clinic was closed on Tuesdays, Wednesdays and Thursdays. Outside the clinic, with the engine running, it was decided that the only thing they could do was to take Harold to his house, make him comfortable, and ring for a doctor.

*

The bay was a crescent, lined with massive rocks. On the eastern flank the rocks jutted out a hundred metres into the ocean. Martin stood near its tip, deep water on both sides, conscious of the swells surging in great unbroken curves past him and into the bay, towards the small beach. Gordon was reeling in his fourth fish in twenty minutes. The swell thumped into the rocks directly below, sending up a plume of spray. Storm clouds lumbered at them from the south.

'Never turn your back to the swell,' Gordon had told him the day before. Martin reeled in his line, letting the surge lift the rig up and over the rocks. But his eyes were on Daniel. He'd left him with Sally and Rachel on the beach, waxing his board.

Daniel was in his wetsuit now, knee-deep, his board riding the foam near the shore. He launched himself at the first rush of white water, arms flailing. It was only a small, broken wave, but Daniel lost his balance and the board speared up and into the air, its white belly glinting.

Martin turned around and Gordon gave him the thumbs up. He was watching Daniel too. Martin reached into the bucket at his feet for another cockle. While he was re-baiting, Daniel got past the first low break and headed for the second. The main break. The swell that thumped and sucked with such force that Martin could feel the vibrations through the dense granite beneath his feet.

For twenty minutes the boy struggled to get past the break as Martin willed him on, holding his breath each time Daniel was sucked under, releasing it only when his son came up for air. Finally, the boy was being drawn towards a glassy wall of water. He paddled furiously at the wave, then

Martin lost him for an agonising moment as the line of swell erased Daniel from view and then the gleaming belly of the board crested the wave, whacked down onto the smooth water behind it and Daniel was safe now, past the break, heading towards them.

Daniel looked around, exhausted. Martin waved to his son and Daniel waved back and Martin felt all his combativeness drain from him like it was a tubful of water and someone had found the plug.

Gordon was at his side now, his line wound in. 'He's gonna be okay,' said Gordon. 'He's gonna turn out fine.'

Martin turned to him, met his eyes and nodded and there was a redness and moistness about Gordon's eyes but it might just have been the wind and the salt.

*

The next day, on the drive back home, Martin stopped at his old school. He hoisted himself over the low fence and Rachel and Daniel tagged along a few paces behind as he cut through the playground. He was heading for the edge of the oval where the class of '86 had planted their trees on graduation.

As soon as he rounded the old arts and crafts building he could see something was wrong but he kept on, his head jerking from side to side as he tried to get his bearings. When he reached the middle of the oval he stopped and waited for Rachel and Daniel to catch up. He turned to them and stretched out a hand to the edge of the field. A long industrial shed sat where the sugar gums had been.

'They've cut me tree down,' he said, mock-humorously, feeling a quiver in his lip.

Rachel gave a hesitant smile. She rested a hand on his elbow. 'I'm sorry, honey,' she said.

'Well, I guess it beats finding it stunted or half dead,' said Martin.

Daniel smiled and then gave a laugh and Martin hesitated for just a second and then joined in with his son, loud and deep.

Lives Less Valuable

Sergeant Simon Hastings – thick forearms, face like a mug shot, a voice full of gravel. Looking at him now, I was aware of how much I'd missed the company of men. The sense of fraternity. We walked into the Colac Hotel, shoulder to shoulder. At the bar, two clapped-out bikies, flying their colours, scowled and looked away.

A beer in one hand, a forkful of peppered steak halfway to his mouth in the other, he paused. 'You just have to take what you can from this job,' he said, and took a slug of beer to wash down the meat, then looked closely at me. He had a way of slowing conversation down and looking you in the eye, gauging your reactions. 'You know what I take?' he continued.

'No,' I said, leaning towards my own glass of beer.

'Little glimpses of lives less valuable than mine.'

I blinked. We stared at each other.

'That helps?' I said at last.

'You'd be surprised.' Hastings took another forkful of steak, chewed it slowly. 'You'd be very surprised.'

I didn't press him. Two weeks into the job and something similar was already working its way into me. The lives of the people we investigated seemed so disjointed, their personalities and characters so twisted out of shape, it made my own life seem full of symmetry and purpose.

I'd never been inside the Colac before. Polished jarrah boards, but everything else spoke of ambulances at four am – plastic chairs, bamboo ashtrays, tables bolted to the floorboards. Nothing that could maim if thrown. Faded portraits of horses hung above the pool table in the far corner of the room.

'Whatdya think of it?' asked Hastings, turning to follow my gaze.

There are places you know instinctively to avoid, and this was one of them. The Colac was a throwback to an uglier time. It had escaped the boom of the mid 2000s that had cut a swathe of concrete and glass through Port Adelaide. This was the last bastion of what, in one of my sociology lectures in my previous life, I would've called 'the disaffected'.

'I've seen more inviting jails,' I said. At the other end of the room, a topless barmaid took money from a man in boots, shorts and singlet covered in dust. The shadows under her eyes looked painted on, even from fifteen metres away. I picked a fishbone out of my mouth, studied it.

'I'm gonna have to work on you, aren't I?' said Hastings.

'What do you mean?'

He ignored my question. 'I went to uni too, you know,' he said.

'Yeah?'

'Well, for a year and a half.'

'What'd you do?'

The bandanaed bikies moved to a pool table in the far corner. The taller of the two picked up a pool cue and inspected the tip, then tightened it between his thumb and forefinger.

'Engineering.' He stared into his beer. 'Got talked into it. Taught me always to trust my gut.'

'What happened?' I asked. The other bikie slammed in the mechanism of the pool table and the balls thundered into its belly.

'Couldn't hack it. The maths. Fourier equations. Jesus!' One of the bikies cracked the balls apart. Hastings looked at me again. 'How many jails have you seen?'

'Just the one,' I admitted. One was enough. 'Yatala. They gave me the tour.' I picked at a chip.

'What'd you think?'

I shook my head, remembering the smell of disinfectant and the vacant expressions on the faces of warders and prisoners.

'I am gonna have to work on you,' he said, looking me in the eye. 'You're the sort who thinks jail's not the answer and you're right,' he continued, leaning in, 'but for the wrong reason.'

I stared back at him.

'I bet you think jails can't rehabilitate men like that.' He pointed over his shoulder at the bikies. 'That all they can do is deter.'

I nodded.

Hastings placed his knife and fork neatly on his plate. 'You gotta understand the psychology of these pricks. Control freaks, bullies. Jail's a dream-come-true for them.' He shrugged his shoulders. 'Well, some of them, anyway.'

*

As far as Alice was concerned, I'd sold out. Sold out my principles, though God knows what they were supposed to be. The principles she thought I *should* have? The same ones she thought we *shared?* A fair go for all; individual rights tempered by the social contract; open, transparent government. Somehow, none of that seemed to fit with my new job.

I dangled my legs over the edge of the wharf, where a tatty twin-deck cruiser disgorged tourists. A cloud of diesel smoke wafted by and I held my breath, felt a wave of nausea come and go.

'See any dolphins?' someone called out from the wharf.

Maybe it was some sort of pre-midlife crisis. Thirty-eight. No kids. I'd been comfortably employed as a lecturer in sociology at the University of Adelaide. Classic redbrick art-deco buildings, a leafy campus, the museum, gallery and library just a few hundred metres away on North Terrace.

One of the cruiser stewards strolled down the gangway and onto the wharf, a can of Coke in hand.

Of the path my life was taking on North Terrace I had begun to think *Why this?* and then its corrosive corollary, *Why not something else?* Once you begin that, it's hard to stop.

So I threw it all in for a job at the Port Adelaide police station. Intelligence analyst. Senior intelligence analyst, coordinating the gang-related-crime taskforce. I always knew I'd be good at this, interpreting statistics and finding patterns in qualitative data. Could do it with my eyes closed.

*

I suspected Alice was struggling, as I was, to maintain an interest in life with no prospect of children. What does it mean that the sweetest, brightest memory I have is of eating a hamburger on the coarse, granitic sand at Port Elliot as a twenty-year-old with Alice beside me and the bay washed an early-evening purple? That I can no longer find a simple pleasure that fills me the way that did?

Anyway, the social contract between us never included the pills she's been taking for the last eighteen months to deaden the pain. The pills have made her closed up, remote. I didn't sign up for that.

When I got home from work I noticed the Robinsons had put an old blackwood dresser on their verge for council collection. I mentioned it to Alice as I rummaged in the pantry for the instant coffee, finding it behind a litter of herbal teas. 'Thinking of bringing it in,' I said.

'What for?'

'Thought I might do it up. Could put it in the spare room.'

Alice didn't reply.

*

I found the fieldwork fascinating. The day after a raid on a property, after the labs had been busted, the guns seized, the cannabis stashed for destruction, Hastings and I would drive out to Adelaide's northern struggle-belt of $120,000 houses, baked earth, three generations of long-term-unemployed living under the same roof, a pitbull chained to a star picket banged into the middle of a leafless backyard that would turn into a quagmire in winter.

A week after the Colac Hotel, Hastings took me on a 'mopping-up' exercise out to Smithfield Plains, past the market gardens and sewage works, the morning sun hazing the window. Constable Dale Simpson rode in the back seat. She reminded me of one of my social work students – a plain girl who'd dropped out halfway through her degree. There was a restlessness about her that you don't often see in a woman.

'This is the one,' said Hastings, pulling up outside an ugly, besser-block house at the end of a dead-end road. Its windows were lined from the inside with alfoil. The carcass of a mid-eighties Commodore festered in the front yard, its axles resting on bricks, a kid with a buzz cut and army trousers on the doorstep. He turned when he saw us, rapped on the door, yelled out, 'Mum. Pigs are here.'

*

Constable Simpson and I barely said a word to each other on the drive to my house. She stared straight ahead the whole way. I was so distracted I mounted the kerb trying to park and then the clank and grind of gears and the screech of kerb on hubcap, but I didn't care, didn't care and the key in my hand and my hand on the handle and my shoulder against the door and the bare boards of the hallway glistening with end-of-day light and Simpson on the floor with her skirt awry, legs apart, amid the gain and give of finger, lip and tongue.

And the terrible afterward. The slack, damp skin. A red-rimmed, raw unhappiness.

*

Alice's eight-year-old nephew, Brad, is having a sleepover. He's a nice kid, but bemused as I am about his presence in our quiet house. We're on our best behaviour and our happiness feels forced. There's a gravity to our lightness.

After dinner the three of us play cards in the kitchen until the phone calls Alice away. I teach Brad the significance of pairs, straights and flushes and we get in a couple of games of poker before Alice comes back, the exhaustion of talking to her mother written all over her face. She sees the matchsticks we're using as money, gives me a 'Really!' and a raised eyebrow and bustles him off for a shower and bed.

When he's safely asleep I go into the spare room to watch him breathe. It's a warm night. The Robinsons' dresser is against the wall, near his bed. A shadow moves on the wall above Brad's head and I step forward, see it's a red-back, and squash it with one of his bedtime books.

Alice is horrified.

'Can you give me a hand?' I ask, and she comes into the bedroom with me. We each take an end and carry the dresser out the back door and into the garage. On the way back to the house, on our perfectly square little patch of lawn, I stop and pull her to me. 'You're shivering,' she says. The night sky is as clear and hard as china-black lacquer. A billion stars burn away indifferently and I have a feeling that something bad will happen soon, or perhaps has already begun.

The Eight-Hundred-Dollar Cat

Small acts of rebellion. It was the creed his grandmother had lived by. Dead ten months now, she'd turned up to all the meetings of the Port Adelaide Heritage Trust, written dozens of letters to the local paper, and handed out bumper stickers at the Art at the Hart Festival: 'Save our Port'.

But none of it had come to anything. The developers had moved in, aided and abetted by the heavyweights on the Labor front bench, and the result was there, staring Ian in the face as he surveyed the harbour from the Birkenhead Bridge.

Late afternoon. The light was perfect. High cirrocumulus to the west in a fine, herringbone pattern. A golden day, late spring. Ian quickly set up his tripod, shot another roll of the wharves, the two old tugboats nuzzling alongside the bridge, the yachts mirrored in the glassy water. Beside him his younger sister, Rachel, leant on the railing of the bridge.

'Nanna's anniversary in six weeks,' she said, watching him as he swapped camera bodies, preferring Kodachrome 64 to capture the tones of the light-washed harbour, the sun pissing away its golden bounty on the shabby buildings.

'Why the fuck do you still bother with film?' she asked. Rust-coloured hair, red lips, a mouthful of perfect white teeth. She'd inherited Nanna's disposition – her default position was anger. Ian sometimes felt like his default was to default. His teachers had told him he was slow, but the world had always seemed to press in on him so firmly that he had to shut most of it out. He preferred to focus on the aesthetics of things.

'Nothing beats film,' he said. 'When they make a twenty-five megapixel camera I can afford, I'll change. Until then...'

*

Ian's new client, Jonathan, wanted 'a visual reminder' of his efforts to develop the Port – a trophy to commemorate the obscene wads of money he'd made.

Their first meeting was on the wharf alongside Hart's Mill, the gloriously dilapidated structure towering over them. On the other side of the river, the man-made mountains of apartments – concrete and steel and stained pine masquerading as Western red cedar. The apartments sold to speculators with no intention of actually living there, with no intention of doing anything but selling at a profit. Bedrooms without windows. A suburb without people.

'They'll cook in those dog boxes in summer,' Ian said as they looked across at Jonathan's achievement, testing him.

'Fuck 'em,' Jonathan replied, a watch the size of an ashtray glinting in the sun.

Jonathan was specific about the artwork. He had a space on the wall of his sitting room that would be perfect. He gave Ian the exact measurements and then, on an impulse, invited him to his Burnside mansion.

*

Jonathan poured whisky into heavy crystal glasses. 'Browns, blues and an overall golden cast,' he said as he poured. 'I want you to capture the way it looks in early-morning light.' He passed Ian his glass, took a sip from his own. 'So that it matches the decor,' he added, gesturing with his free hand to take in his chesterfields and polished hardwood floor.

A smoky, yellow-eyed cat walked into the room and rubbed itself against Ian's leg.

'He doesn't usually do that to strangers,' said Jonathan.

'I feel very privileged.' Ian screwed up his face. He didn't much like cats.

'You should,' said Jonathan, missing Ian's tone. He picked up the cat and stroked it. 'Cost me eight hundred dollars.'

*

Ian worked from photos, building layer upon layer of pigment and beeswax onto the canvas. 'Urban Monstrosity in Morning Light' became his private title for the work, but he tried to find beauty in the botched architecture, in its naked insistence, in its grand failure to concede anything to its surroundings.

Halfway through the project his lover wrote something on a scrap of paper and stuck it to the wall, beside the canvas: 'Poverty is a straightjacket, made to order.'

'What does that mean?' Ian asked.

'Figure it out yourself.'

*

He arrived ten minutes early on the day of installation. Knocked on the imposing twin five-metre-tall black-lacquered doors. Jonathan's wife opened the door and propped it open. Tracksuited, dead-straight hair, fifteen years younger than Jonathan, she smelt faintly of sweat.

'Working out,' she said, smiling at him. 'He's in there.' She pointed, curved her finger backwards to indicate he should turn right at the end of the hallway. 'The living room.'

Ian went back to his van and returned with the canvas, stretched and ready to hang. He found Jonathan sitting on one of the chesterfields, glass in hand, talking on his mobile. He waved for Ian to place the canvas on the ground. Ian saw that the space he'd thought was his had been taken over by a monstrously large, flat-screen television. He propped the canvas against the wall, below the screen. Jonathan kept talking, waved him out of the room.

In the hallway, Ian looked at the back of the house and saw a deck through the floor-to-ceiling glass, a backyard beyond it. He walked out. Before him, an impossibly neat garden. Everything that could be standardised – roses, lavender, lilly pilly – had been. In the distance, the Adelaide skyline. Beyond that he could see, faintly, the twin towers of the Torrens Island power station. The Port itself was difficult to make out. But not for much longer, if the plans he'd seen for the third stage of development were correct. It would ruin the Port.

He looked down. Jonathan's eight-hundred-dollar cat, curled asleep on the second tier of decking. It was the anniversary of Nanna's death tomorrow, and the family would gather at the Semaphore Hotel to drink a beer or two to her memory.

Ian unzipped himself and felt the cool, clean Burnside air on his penis as he began pissing on the cat.

You Matter to God

He swung the big car slowly into the church car park. At this empty, quiet hour, the gravel crunched under the wheels as he pulled the Falcon around and parked in front of the sign. YOU MATTER TO GOD! *Someone had scribbled beneath it in black,* BUT EVERYONE ELSE THINKS YOUR A FUCKWIT! *Next to him, in the passenger seat, the woman sighed and he wondered what she was thinking.*

He stared ahead, her profile on the edge of his vision, and thought again of the image Robert had shown him. The way it flipped from young girl to old woman if you concentrated on it. He knew exactly how that felt. It wasn't long ago that he could flip from hero to zero in the space of a day. Wake up knowing he was renowned in the district as a fearless surfer and footballer (retired), then drink himself to sleep knowing he was a useless bum, pissing his days away.

'Do you ever wish,' he asked, 'that things had turned out better?'

She wound her window down and the smell of eucalypt, astringent and warm, swamped the car. 'You shouldn't be so hard on yourself,' she said. 'Really, there's nothing wrong with you. People want to like you. You should let them.'

For a minute or so he said nothing, then reached across the vastness of the Falcon and took her hand.

*

The scrape of wood against floorboards woke me and I lay there until a rattling noise came from the kitchen. Geoff, the old bastard, helping himself to my coffee.

I propped myself up, dragged the curtain across the grey morning and let it fall back into place. It had been a bad night. The first call-out had come at two am, the second around three, and sleep not until five or so. And here I was, my clock radio figuring 7:13 and another overcast Victor Harbor day to deal with.

I got out of bed, threw on a tracksuit and my denim jacket over the top and stumbled into the kitchen. Geoff was at the knotty pine table, hunkered over a large mug of coffee. I could smell the sugar from the doorway; he must've put half the bloody jar in.

'Morning,' I said, and he grunted back. Geoff was a cranky bugger at the best of times. The rumour was he'd thrown away close to a million on a get-rich-quick super scheme that turned out dodgy. Buggered up his retirement plans.

'Heard you get in,' he said, cradling his mug to keep his hands warm.

I flicked the kettle and put a large spoonful of coffee into one of the 'God's Waiting Room' cups I'd nicked from the footy club. 'Sorry. Tried to be quiet.'

I'd sublet the front room to Geoff three months ago, not by choice. I had responsibilities now that Josh's mum, Julie, was sick. I was aiming to save enough to put a deposit on a house for the two of us. Me and Josh. Julie too if she'd have me back. Something simple. A weatherboard cottage in Goolwa perhaps.

He was a miserable bastard but he didn't drink or talk much, which suited me fine. And he kept an eye on Josh while I was working nights. I stirred a big spoonful of sugar into my coffee and sipped the bittersweet brew.

'How was Josh?' I asked.

'Fine. Not a peep.' He rubbed his hands together. 'Fuck this house is cold.'

There was nothing new to say to that. I took my coffee into Josh's room, his face unblemished and pure in the weak morning light. The room reeked of piss. I groaned and gently rocked him awake.

'Josh,' I said. 'Get up mate. You've wet the bed again.'

While he had a shower I stripped his bed and dumped everything in the laundry.

Dr Ferguson had prescribed Tofranil for the bed-wetting and nodded when I told him Josh was having problems fitting in at school. He handed me the script and said, 'This should help with that too.'

'What do you mean?' I asked. He had bushy eyebrows, a red bowtie, and a way of holding himself as if he was expecting a television crew to appear from nowhere and turn him into a celebrity. He was about my height – six-one, but slack-shouldered, flabby. Wouldn't last thirty seconds on a footy field but what did that matter. I was on his turf.

'You're a single parent household?' he asked.

'Yeah, so what?' Josh was eyeing off the bowl of jellybeans on Ferguson's desk. He hadn't offered, and I hoped Josh wouldn't take one uninvited.

'Nothing,' he said. 'We just see a lot of that around here.'

'His mum's got cancer.' I hadn't wanted to say that, but there it was. My lower lip trembled.

He frowned. 'I'm sorry,' he said, not looking at me.

I looked at the script, keen to change the subject. 'Tofranil. So, why should this,' I squinted at the prescription, 'help with school?'

'It's an antidepressant.'

'What does he need that for?'

He looked at Josh and in front of him, right in bloody front of him, said, 'He's got what I would call a sad brain.'

I felt like punching him.

I never felt comfortable in the schoolyard but the mums had been and gone, so I sucked in the dread, parked the Falcon and walked Josh to his classroom, a demountable surrounded by scraggy paperbarks and tea-trees. I leant down to give him a kiss and he said 'See ya Dad', then slid his bag under a bench and walked slowly inside, where the teacher was calling the roll. Arriving after the mums made it difficult for Josh, who rarely got invites to other kids' houses, but at least I didn't have to put up with them not looking at me, not acknowledging me, all of them knowing who I was, the family I came from, and how far I'd fallen.

The sky was spitting. I turned to go and saw one of Josh's classmates running towards me, followed by his dad. The boy threw his bag and it slid five metres into the side of the classroom, settling perfectly under the bench. I raised an eyebrow to his dad, a short, stocky man with a thin stubble on his head and something Arabic tattooed on his forearm. He shook his head and we both laughed. He had a shirt with 'Do I Know You?' in big letters across it and, below that, two cartoon dogs, one sniffing the other's arse. I wondered what the Arabic meant.

'How's he going?' I asked.

'Brayden?' He screwed up his face, shook his head. 'Doesn't like it much. What about yours?'

'Josh? He's alright. Finding it a bit hard to make friends though.'

We chatted about teachers and mums and how neither of our boys had been invited to a birthday party this year. I looked at his shirt again – no surprises there. So I invited him to drop Brayden over for a play the next day. 'Too much on my plate today,' I said.

'Yeah?' He raised an eyebrow.

'Work,' I replied. 'Night-shift security. Rental properties, holiday homes, businesses.' I hesitated, thought, *Fuck it.* 'And I've got a meeting with my probation officer this afternoon.'

He nodded, didn't blink. Passed the test.

*

I pointed the Falcon at Goolwa, twenty kilometres to the east. At

Middleton I stopped at a cafe and bought an iced coffee and sat at a scuffed-up plastic table as a Greyhound bus pulled up. A pudgy little bloke in a green and white checked shirt got up from the next table as the passengers clambered out, all stretches and groans. He stood there, waiting, and then a girl came out of the bus, about twenty, no hips, skinny as a rat. She went straight for him, hugged him, and belted out a smile that could save your life. And here's me, wishing I was him. That quick.

I got back in the Falcon and kept going. Goolwa. A flat little tick of a town, its head buried in the bank of the River Murray. Inside Vanessa's office, I summoned up enough of my old charm to wink at the new girl behind the counter and she smiled back, hesitantly. She'd probably already heard half a dozen stories about me from the bad old days.

'Vanessa in?'

She nodded and I poked my head around the door of my sister's office and gave her a 'G'day sis'. My younger sister and only sibling.

'Hi Mark,' she said off-handedly, sitting at her desk, a manila folder thick with papers in front of her. She was tapping some numbers into a calculator, one eye on the phone. 'How's Josh?'

'He's fine.' I stood there, wanting to ask for another ten grand, my share of our father's inheritance. At least that was how I saw it. He'd cut me out of his will when he'd dropped in unannounced one day and found me climbing the walls, drenched with sweat, fighting the DTs, right in the middle of a three-hour rant about kissing God and wanting to die. It was too much for him. He'd always been a religious man, my father. And it probably didn't help that he knew he was dying.

He's been dead two years now. When do you stop wishing you could undo things that have been and gone?

'And Julie?' Vanessa stopped what she was doing with the calculator and brushed some lint off her jacket.

'Dunno,' I said. 'She's got cancer. Not that well I guess.'

Vanessa shook her head, partly in sympathy for Julie; partly, I suspect, in disapproval of me. I caught a glimpse of a portrait of a woman propped against the wall behind her. The face resembled Vanessa's.

'Here's the list,' she said, and the right moment to ask the ten-thousand-dollar question was gone. Down to business. I checked through the list of unattended properties I'd have to drive by that night. Alongside a couple there were instructions like 'water the front lawn' and 'replace cracked louvre in bathroom window'. Goolwa Realty offered a complete service. I took the list and left.

On the way home I stopped at the chemist and picked up the Tofranil. Then back home for some breakfast and a retreat to bed to make up what I'd lost the night before. The doona was cold at first against my skin. I drifted off, thinking of Julie.

*

I picked up Josh from school and we walked up the hill to the Baptist church where Robert, my probation officer and counsellor, had his office. Alongside the old sandstone church was a newer, low-roofed building with a concrete access ramp already fretting at the edges. Inside, it had the feel of a third-rate gym, with a concrete floor and two table tennis tables set up in the middle, a doubles match taking place on one of them. Two girls – one with braces, the other with pigtails – playing a couple of skinny, pale boys.

At the other table, another young lad was playing Robert. The ball flew off the table and Robert cut it back with such spin that his opponent's return fired into the base of the net. Robert put his bat down on the table, spun the wheel of his chair and rolled over to where Josh and I stood.

'Have a game if you like,' he said to Josh, who said 'Okay' and picked up the bat and hit the first one straight into the net. Robert turned to me, shook my hand, said, 'Good to see you, Mark', like he meant it.

He glided into his office and I closed the door behind us. Robert had been a big man once and still had presence, even in a wheelchair. It was about a year and a half now since the crash that had killed his wife, left him paraplegic, and saw him pensioned from the police force and turning to God. 'You know,' he'd said on our first meeting, 'that was probably the only time that week I wasn't pissed while I was driving,' and he'd shaken his head in disbelief and stared straight ahead and I'd wondered how this was going to work. A God-fearing, remorseful, depressed ex-cop to counsel me.

But somehow it had. He was off the grog now and I hadn't touched anything stronger than coffee with a shot of rum since I'd given up the hash and the speed and the rest of it when I was picked up at a random breath-testing station last July and busted for possession.

'How's it going?' he asked. He had grey hair, cut short, and eyebrows like steel wool. In front of him was a sheet of paper and a manila folder with my name written across the top in thick black texta. He was tapping the folder with a pen and the simple action made his forearm ripple with muscle and tendons. Wheelchairs were good for that, at least.

'Alright,' I said. We talked a bit about Josh and his mum and about my plans to buy a cottage one day. I didn't mention Vanessa and the money I felt she owed me.

'And what about the AA meetings?'

I shrugged my shoulders, avoided his gaze. It was a condition of my probation that I attended meetings in Goolwa. I hadn't gone at all last month. Seven or eight earnest, older men, sitting on plastic chairs in the community hall, sharing their pain. 'It's not for me,' I said at last.

Robert nodded his head. 'I tried it myself,' he said. 'As you know.'

My turn to nod.

'I couldn't get it to work either,' he continued. 'The constant vigilance...' His voice tapered off. A shriek of laughter came from the other room, then the sound of a bat striking a table.

'They were always telling me addiction is a disease,' I said. For some reason, I found it easy to talk to Robert about this stuff. Maybe because he was older than me. It was nearly fifteen years since I'd done my knee and had to give up footy. Fifteen years since I'd had a coach and a captain, older men taking an interest in my game.

'That's what you're supposed to think,' said Robert. 'But it's more than that. Addiction,' he said, 'is a symptom.' He paused and looked at me and I could see he'd been thinking about this, thinking about what he was going to say. From the other room came the steady click-click, click-clack of a rally.

'A symptom of what?' I asked.

He gripped the arms of his wheelchair as if he had forgotten his injury and was set to raise himself up. 'A thousand squandered opportunities to develop your character.' A faint tremor rippled across his face as if a bomb had gone off somewhere deep inside him and then he leant back in his chair. 'There,' he said, almost apologetically. 'I've said it. That's what I've been thinking lately.'

I realised then that he needed me as much as I needed him. Or perhaps it was just *the role* he needed – to be mentoring someone. And what he'd just said was exactly what a born-again ex-cop who'd accidentally killed his wife in a car crash would say to someone like me. But that didn't mean it was wrong.

Robert asked me what I wanted to do with the next ten years of my life and I told him how I'd actually been pretty good at school. Believe it or not. Not a top student, but I'd excelled at sport, enjoyed biology. I was going to be a park ranger when I left school. Would've loved that – knew the Coorong like the back of my hand. The lagoons, the birds, the beaches. Still did.

'You know you could still do that if you wanted,' said Robert, and it almost sounded like he was jealous. There are worse things than not having qualifications. Not having legs, for instance.

'I suppose I could,' I said, almost off-handedly.

Towards the end of our session Robert handed me a black and white image on a card. A young woman if you looked at it one way, an old woman if you stared long and hard enough.

'Get anything from that?' asked Robert.

I shook my head.

'Nothing at all?'

I'd had enough. I was thinking again of the Tofranil and sad brains and how I'd have to take some of those pills to test them before I gave them to Josh. I flicked the card back at him and it spun in the air and landed on his desk. 'Nothing,' I said.

He sat there, wanting something more from me.

'What do *you* get from *this*?' I asked him, but he didn't get what I meant and began talking about how the mentoring had helped him to shift the focus away from himself after his wife had died, and I said, 'No, I mean, what do you get from all *this*?' And I swung my arm around to include the room we were in, the church next door, the picture of Jesus on the wall.

'One day,' he said, 'I'll read you something from the Bible.'

I grimaced. 'Won't work on me.'

He laughed. 'Yeah, maybe you're right. It's like the warnings they give on diet plans – conditions apply.'

'Yeah,' I said. 'Results may vary.'

*

After a dinner of Josh's favourite, sausages with white bread, mashed potato and sweet corn, I took one of Josh's anti-bed-wetting, anti-sad-brain pills. A tiny, sky-blue thing. I flicked between the current affairs shows, hoping for light relief. By then I was feeling slightly dazed, as though the world were covered in cottonwool. Dr Ferguson had said two pills a day.

After I'd put Josh to bed I put on my work clobber, grabbed my steel-cased don't-fuck-with-me torch, took the second pill and said goodnight to Geoff. 'Call me if you need me,' I said. He grunted, eyes glued to the screen as some American cop in an expensive suit lifted up the corner of a tarp and gagged.

I pointed the Falcon at Goolwa for the second time that day. I always began my patrol in Goolwa, working my way slowly back home through Middleton and Port Elliott to Victor Harbor.

I drove in a daze, jolting into North Goolwa when the road banked the River Murray and its sounds and smells washed over me through the open window. The great salty drain of inland Australia. At school we'd known the Murray-Darling as one of the world's great river systems. We'd done a class project – had stacked up its length, catchment area, annual discharge and so on against the Nile, the Mississippi, the Amazon and the Yangtze. The Murray-Darling had come last in every category, but that didn't matter, it was ours. Anyway, we were used to coming last.

My job was simple. I had to drive by each of the unattended holiday homes and businesses on my list, stop outside each one, do a visual check for intruders. Unexplained lights, broken windows. Get out only if necessary. Break and enters were reasonably common in the off-season and you could get squatters any time of the year.

The first house on my list was a kit home, all HardiPlank and aluminium windows on a narrow block near the river, flanked by empty houses managed by other estate agents, owned by Adelaide people who came down only when the weather was good. There's no Neighbourhood Watch in a holiday town.

I killed the engine and listened. The second pill was beginning to take hold, the cottonwool getting thicker. The listening turned to slack-mouthed staring until something jolted me and I started up the car and headed for the next property on my list.

By midnight I'd done all of Goolwa and Port Elliott and the seaside part of Victor Harbor and my face was numb. I didn't give a fuck. It was like someone had removed that part of my brain with all the soft bits, like the bits you use when you look at your son and want to hold him close so that all the bad things that got hold of you won't get hold of him.

My mobile rang and I pulled over. A call-out. 18 Dennis Drive, Port Elliott. I pointed the car to the east.

*

I knew the house well. Young and rich, the owner came down from Adelaide on weekends and threw all-nighters with plenty of girls and drugs. There had been complaints and

I'd been involved once or twice. Didn't like the prick.

I parked outside his house. Two-storey. Near new. Across the road from parklands and his million-dollar view of Horseshoe Bay. I sat there with the engine off and the doors locked, just in case. There was no sign of torchlight, no trees to hide behind, so I wound down the window and listened.

When I was sure there was no one around, I called the security company and told the woman who answered where I was. 'Probably just a false alarm,' I said.

'Well, be careful, love.' I could see her sitting in an office somewhere in Adelaide, a blanket draped over her knees, a crossword and a hot chocolate beside her.

I let myself in the side gate and the back door was ajar. Bad sign. I stopped and listened. Nothing. I clicked my torch on and held it in the overhand grip, ready to pivot it down on someone's head if I needed to. I walked quietly through the downstairs rooms, turning on each light as I went. Then upstairs and into the main living room. It was a mess. The cleaner hadn't been in since the last party. I moved slowly, just in case. Room by room, leaving each light on as I went. Nothing.

I returned to the living room and to the wall-to-wall, floor-to-ceiling glass doors that looked out over the ocean. I wondered how it would feel to own such a house. Would it make you stand taller, straighter; would it allow you to look more people in the eye?

The floor and coffee table were covered with empty Crownies and wine bottles and the stale beer smelt like my youth and the football club. I sat down and felt something hard beneath me. An iPod. Josh would love it. I rubbed the smooth cold case between my fingers.

Just inside the glass doors stood a telescope. On a clear day you'd be able to see the Coorong from here. Something about that filled me with a sadness so deep and swift that it cut through the Tofranil. I let the iPod drop to the floor. Josh would soon be old enough to see me as I was.

*

After that I must've gone on autopilot for a while because I found myself approaching the car park above my old surf beach, Waitpinga. I parked overlooking the water and the Bluff loomed behind me. The swell looked mean. I closed my eyes and, even with the drugs gripping my brain, shutting me down, the roar and crash of the surf filled my head. I was being tossed about by massive, dark walls of water. And I wanted to be out there, at the edge of the break, my skin burning cold, the waves thumping the drug out of my system. In the state I was in, I knew I probably wouldn't survive.

And then I felt something, almost with the force of memory ... that I was empty. That there was nothing left inside me. It scared the shit out of me. I wound down the window, stuck my head into the wind and the darkness and shouted, 'My name is Mark South', over and over.

I stumbled out of the Falcon with the bottle of Tofranil, leaning into the wind. I threw up into a bin, then unscrewed the lid of the bottle and upended the lot. Back in the car, I turned off my mobile and headed for home. My night was done.

The next morning I dropped off Josh and went for a drive with Julie, past the bare hills, to the north of town. We drove mainly in silence. As I approached the outskirts of Para West I swung the big car slowly into the church car park.

Girl, Reflected

You wake up with terror surging through your veins and you don't know why. There was a dream: something to do with high school friends and how you lost them, one by one. You've erased most of it from your mind. You had to cut yourself off – you hated who you were and you knew they'd never let you be anyone else. You'd always be their fool. They needed you for that. At least, that's how it seemed at the time.

The train crosses the river. You keep an eye on the water. The boats and their reflections, the derelict boat yards, an occasional dolphin cruising the murky waters of the Port River for prey, slumming it with the lead-addled bream.

You're still reeling from the news.

She stands in the aisle of the train and light reflects from her in every direction. Visual messages encoded in photons, streaming away. Some of them shoot out into the dark huddle of early morning. They hit the window of the train at exactly the right angle and reflect back at you and there she is, projected against a dark factory wall, now ghostlike against the grey sky, now bright against a row of pines. Bright ... ghostly ... bright ... the train rushes on.

You pretend you're looking out at the wasteland hurtling by but your eyes are fixed on her face. She's staring out as well, and it's as if she's looking right back at you. You know you'll see her again in the evening on the 5.13 from Adelaide to Glanville.

Two rows behind you, Bill sits among his fellow citizens, wearing the six-hundred-dollar suit he treated himself to when he was promoted to Manager, Customer Services. The public service has been good to him. He's looking at the girl standing in the aisle. He takes her into his mind, slowly undresses her, turns and bends her this way and that. After a while he tires of it, lets her go, opens a book.

Three rows behind you sits Bronwyn. Twelve months ago she lost her husband and her only child, her son. Her husband took him too far out in the surf one vile, chaotic day at Goolwa and couldn't get him back in before all the air in his thirteen-year-old lungs had been replaced by salt water. He killed himself three days later. You know nothing of this.

At the terminal, your fellow passengers spill from the train like blood cells, surging through the turnstiles and into the city, transfusing the day.

The connecting bus is late. You wait, urgently, wanting to talk to the girl in the op-shop cardie and bright purple trousers standing beside you. You want to tell her to be careful about who she talks to. But you don't. How could you?

When the bus comes you sit two rows behind her. At the lights on Pulteney Street an electrician's van pulls up alongside, large tinted windows running down the side. The photons do their work and the girl in the cardie is cast into the back of the van. She sits just two rows away from you while her doppelganger slouches among cables, ties and rolls of tape.

Last night you found out that your best friend's daughter has gone missing. The world has changed during the night. You no longer recognise it.

Conditional Release

On his way from Geraldton through clapped-out mulga to the remote gold-mining town of Meekatharra, Dan stopped for morning tea at the welfare office in Mullewa – a converted, asbestos-lined house beside a vacant lot, across the road from the courthouse. 'Location, location, location,' he could hear Amanda's father saying. Sarcasm was one of his ex-father-in-law's strong points.

He stayed just long enough, over weak Black & Gold tea and homemade Anzac biscuits, to get the impression he was about to slip off the edge of the world. 'Meeka,' grunted Trevor, the slack-jowled, sixty-something officer in charge, barely looking up from the daily paper. 'Watch out for the dogs.'

Trevor's offsider, Kate, a young social worker from Perth, rolled her eyes. Around her neck she wore a string of beads in various dull shades of ochre. When Dan asked her, she told him they were native seeds, strung together on a cord made from strands of human hair, and he wished he hadn't. A tiny muscle in the corner of her mouth ticked away and Dan could see she wasn't happy with where her four years at uni had landed her. 'Take no notice of Trevor,' she said. 'He hates the place.'

Trevor grunted again and turned a page.

'His son,' explained Kate, 'got beaten up there last year.' She made a face on 'son', as if she thought he'd probably deserved it. Dan raised an eyebrow and took a bite of his crumbly biscuit, wishing he was back in his car, alone, with just the sound of the wind rushing by.

'Ran over someone's dog,' she continued.

'It was an accident,' said Trevor. 'But they dragged him out of his car anyway. Beat the shit out of him.'

*

Cresting the last small hill before Meekatharra, a roadhouse on his right, the streets glary and slick with panes of afternoon light crashing up at him from the wet roads, Dan pumped the brakes, mindful of the road train weighing in behind him. Ninety, eighty, seventy, sixty and he was already well into town and the grill of the road train filled his rear-view mirror. His eyes darted to the road's edge where children of all hues played in puddles of red. He gripped the steering wheel tightly.

Dan pulled up outside the welfare office, the third last building before the road snaked north out of town. He got out, flexed his head from side to side and breathed in the warm stink of summer rain on red earth. On the other side of the road, bordered on all sides by drab, low scrub, a field of asphalt shone crazily in the dying light, basketball backboards against the pale blue horizon. None of them had rings, let alone nets. It took him a couple of seconds to figure out that the constellations of light on the courts were a galaxy of broken glass.

Up the steps to the office and he was about to knock a second time when the door opened. A man in his late thirties, bearded, stared at him like he was about to start shaking his head to whatever Dan might say.

'Graham?' Dan asked. 'Dan, from the Geraldton office.' He held out his hand and Graham opened the door a little wider, wiped his hand on his green King Gees and shook Dan's.

'Pleased to meet ya,' he said. 'Come on in.'

Inside the office he presented Dan with the key to his house and drew a mud map of the town.

'Looks like it's right next to the tip,' said Dan, frowning at the map.

'Yeah, but it's alright,' replied Graham. 'Nice and quiet out there. Just close yer windows when the southerly blows.'

Graham dragged a couple of VBs out of the office fridge in the corner of the room. A couple of beers later, when the conversation had dried up, Dan drove back through town, stopping at the roadhouse to pick up a meal of fish and chips in a cardboard box. Parked outside his new home he killed the engine and sat there in the darkness for longer than he should have, suddenly overwhelmed. Graham had let himself go. Shorts and thongs, a stained T-shirt, matching set of tangled hair and beard. But he looked harmless enough. Perhaps the Geraldton people were wrong.

*

Dan settled quietly into his government-issue house and the work that went with it. The house was thin-walled, asbestos-roofed and a decade or two older than Dan. He took walks in the mornings to get his bearings, and explored the crosshatching of trails around the town dump. At the end of his first week in Meekatharra he threw away the antidepressants he'd been carting around since Amanda had left him six months earlier. By then he had a fair idea of the work and felt he could rise to meet it.

The town was at crisis point. In the previous twelve months, thirty-two of its children had been sent to juvenile detention centres in Perth, across a weary eight-hundred-kilometre stretch of scrub to the south. Everything from joy riding to robbery with violence.

On the day before he'd been sent to Meeka, Dan had been summonsed to the Regional Director's office. Patrick sat in a puffed up leather director's chair, his desk immaculate. 'The magistrate is pissed off,' he explained. 'And Graham's a fuckwit. We don't know what he's doing out there.' Patrick had taken off his glasses, rubbed his forehead and stared out at the pine trees opposite his office. Dan waited. 'Your job,' Patrick continued, 'will be to find some alternatives for these kids. Community service, probation, conditional release orders.' He waved his hands as he spoke, as if trying to conjure up the things he was talking of. 'So the magistrate doesn't have to keep locking the little darlings up.'

Dan nodded.

'And keep an eye on Graham, will you? There's rumours.' Patrick winced and Dan waited for the gossip, but the older man held it in.

*

Dan had to escort a young Aboriginal girl to the girls' prison in Perth. Shania had got two months for stealing a carton of Jim Beam and Cola from the Railway Hotel.

He sat beside her on the plane. She was nearly fifteen, dressed in blue jeans and a yellow top that set off her skin and her gold, streaky, desert-child hair. It was a small jet, a thirty-two-seat Skywest, and the seats were so close their elbows kept touching. She smelt like corn chips. She was shy, so he gave her the book he'd planned to re-read before he remembered, too late, that it ended badly. *They Shoot Horses, Don't They?* Something he'd been dragging around with him from his uni days.

Perth was difficult. On the Saturday morning he found himself at the war memorial overlooking Fremantle, the sun on his back, trying to pick out the limestone villa he'd shared with Amanda. By Sunday afternoon he was glad to be back in Meeka, picking his way through the town dump, looking for old tyres he could take home to grow potatoes in. The light was slanting in from just above the horizon and everything looked softer and prettier, even the piles of rubbish. The drab trees and bushes glowed, each one textured by a thousand tiny shadows.

*

It was Graham's idea to introduce Dan to Andrew Fowler and do a handover of his responsibilities at the same time. He pulled up outside the bottle-o on their way out of town.

'Won't Andrew mind?' asked Dan. 'Isn't he a preacher or something?'

'Ex-preacher,' Graham said, winking at him. 'Fuck no. Likes a beer as much as the next man.'

Fowler's station ran sheep. By Meekatharra standards it was a small outfit, among low hills and breakaways north of the 180-kilometre-long dirt road that ran east to west from Meekatharra to Wiluna. A series of gates lay between the turn-off and the homestead. After his third gate, Dan kept his seatbelt undone as Graham picked his way carefully along the rutted track.

'Don't expect too much,' said Graham as he eased the Holden up to the fourth gate.

Dan got out, unlatched the gate and dragged it across the track, then dragged it back after the car had moved forward. He climbed back in.

'He's a funny bastard.' Graham wiped the sweat from his brow, transferred it to his shirt.

The track forked and then straightened out, with stockyards to their left and a graveyard of machines on their right. Broken-down, cannibalised tractors and utes and at least half a dozen small trucks, mainly old Bedfords. Most of them looked reasonably intact.

'Nothing rusts out here,' said Graham. 'It's too dry. Edge of the desert.' Ahead, Dan could see a low building surrounded by stunted pines. The closer they got to the homestead, the worse it looked.

Graham parked in front of the building and honked his horn. Silence. After a minute or so, Graham popped the boot of the car and came back with two stubbies of VB. He was on his third stubbie when Andrew pulled up on a quad bike in a cloud of dust, an Aboriginal boy of maybe twelve or thirteen holding on behind him. Graham got out of the car, shook Andrew's hand, and introduced him to Dan.

'He's gonna be looking after you from now on,' said Graham to Andrew. 'They've given me the arse.' He burped loudly on 'arse'.

Andrew was a big, wild-eyed man, his thick black hair and beard covered in fine red dust. There was a stiffness about him like something inside him had died. He led the men through the house, the walls grim with dust and the sweat of jackaroos. The floor crunched under Dan as he followed Graham, the carton on his shoulder.

On the back veranda, Graham sat the carton on an overturned washing machine. Andrew wrestled a nest of chairs apart and placed three of them around a hole that had been smashed into the middle of the concrete slab. It had a ring of blackened stones around it and held the remains of a fire. Twenty metres away, the scrub reasserted itself in a dense tangle of bush and grass. It looked snaky and dangerous to Dan.

Dan took it all in. This was it. The only station in the district that Graham had recruited to take in impressionable young offenders on conditional release as an alternative to jail. *Were all the stations like this?*

'Where you from?' asked Andrew, twisting the lid off a stubbie.

'Perth,' said Dan.

'University?'

'Yep,' said Dan. 'I did English and History but found out I didn't want to teach.' He was trying to be expansive. 'I got sick of Perth,' knowing, as he said it, the truth was he'd got sick of himself.

Graham asked Andrew about the season he was having and the two of them talked for a while as if Dan wasn't there. Whenever Dan tried to join in, Andrew became monosyllabic and guarded. The scrub in front of him was all-of-a-piece and hard to look at.

Four beers later they left Andrew on the back veranda. Dan shook hands with the ex-preacher but he didn't rise from his chair.

'See you in a month or two,' said Dan.

'Yep,' said Andrew.

*

Dan took a call from Patrick the next morning.

'How'd it go?' asked Patrick.

'It's a shocker,' said Dan, turning the overhead fan onto 'High' and keeping his voice low in case Graham could hear. 'I wouldn't send a sick dog out there.'

There was a few seconds of silence from the Geraldton end. 'That good, eh?' said Patrick at last. Then, 'Shit. What are we going to do about it?'

Dan told Patrick of the promising leads he'd had in the last week or so. A sheep station to the west of town, owned by a local Aboriginal man. An emu farm near Wiluna. Both had wanted to know more about conditional release and the subsidies that went with each child placed.

'Check 'em out,' said Patrick, 'and get back to me as soon as you can. We've gotta get moving on this before it all blows up.'

'Okay,' said Dan, and waited. He knew what Patrick really wanted. Some evidence to go with the rumours he'd heard himself from one of the police constables – that Graham was rooting some of his welfare clients in exchange for food vouchers, care of the department.

'Anything else?' asked Patrick.

Dan stared at the fan. He had a sudden image of Captain Willard in *Apocalypse Now,* wired and sleepless on a ruined bed. 'Nothing yet,' he said.

'Hmm.' Patrick wasn't convinced. 'Look,' he said, 'I need you to do something for me...'

*

Dan settled into a workable rhythm of keeping mainly to himself during the week and getting shit-faced at any or all of the town's three pubs on Friday and Saturday nights. Sunday mornings he pottered around his yard, watering his potatoes and the tomatoes he'd planted near the septic tank. Light outdoor work helped ease the sense of remorse that would otherwise follow the drinking sessions.

During the week he concentrated on juvenile justice, attending magistrate's court twice a week in Meekatharra. He'd get the charge sheet the afternoon before and drive around town, interviewing the parents, uncles and aunts of the children due in court the next morning, working out the possibilities of fines, good behaviour bonds, probation and community service.

He got to know Shania's family well. Her older sister, Cassie, a slim, handsome girl in her early twenties, was trying to control her five younger siblings, their mother recently dead and their father, a whitefella, on the grog in Port Hedland.

Over a cup of tea on her dusty front veranda, the mullock heaps of the open-cut gold mine rearing up two hundred metres away, they talked about Shania's impending return from the girls' prison in Perth. Cassie wanted her to finish high school. When they'd finished talking, Dan got up. 'Well,' he said. 'We'll give it a go. Have a think about what she might need and let me know.'

*

Later that week, Cassie came to the welfare office and asked to see Dan. He let her in and closed the door, the smell of soap and banana trailing behind her. She had a list for Dan. Three high school textbooks, two school uniforms, pens, notebooks and a school bag.

'Okay,' said Dan. 'We can probably put all this on a voucher.'

As he began writing it out he stole a look at Cassie. She was looking at her hands clasped together between her legs, her wrists riding on the taut red hem of her skirt. She looked up and Dan looked away, signed the order and gently tore it from the book.

'Going to the Commie tonight?' Dan asked and then immediately wished he hadn't. There was something wrong here – the voucher, Cassie, him. He passed her the voucher and she gave a little smile and a nod and got up to leave, straightening her skirt as she did so.

'Might see you there,' Dan said, casually, and let her out. He closed the door and stood there, breathing in deeply as the soap and banana smell faded.

That night he started at the Railway Hotel, playing pool and drinking Swan Draught with a couple of dusty miners. Graham stuck his head in at sundown and looked around. Dan waved him over and bought him a drink.

'Andrew's coming in tonight,' said Graham, opening a packet of chips. 'Staying at my place.'

Dan nodded, remembering Patrick's request.

'So how you findin' Meeka?' asked Graham, offering Dan a chip.

'It's alright,' said Dan.

'You wanna watch out for those dickheads in Geraldton,' said Graham. 'Stitch you up if you give 'em half a chance.' Graham took a long swig of his beer and burped. 'They've forgotten what it's like out here. Things don't work the same.'

Dan nodded.

'Rule number one,' said Graham, dismounting from his stool. 'Make sure you cover your own arse.' He downed his beer and jerked his head towards the west side of town. 'Better go see what's happened to that prick Andrew.'

*

Later, at the Commercial Hotel, Dan bought Cassie a Bundy and coke and stood beside her for a while as they watched a one-dayer on the hotel plasma. The pub was packed and Dan had to put his mouth close to Cassie's ear to make himself heard. Once or twice his arm brushed against hers and his four or five beers made him feel generous and forgiving, even towards himself.

Across the room, he caught occasional glances of Graham and Andrew sitting at a small table in the corner with some Aboriginal girls. The ex-preacher was laughing, his hair combed and curling up at his shoulder.

As Dan was buying another round of drinks, Andrew joined him.

'Good to see you here,' said Andrew. 'Why don't you come over?' He jerked his head towards the back of the room.

'I will,' said Dan, collecting his drinks. He returned to Cassie and stood beside her as Ponting pirouetted and struck the ball to deep square leg. One of Cassie's cousins, a stocky young jackaroo, flashed Dan a smile, took Cassie's hand and began dragging her away.

'Thanks,' she said to Dan over her shoulder and mimed a swimming stroke with her free hand, as if trying to escape her cousin's grasp and return to him. Dan felt a sudden pang of hopefulness and then she was gone.

He watched the end of the over and then moved through the crowd to Andrew and Graham's table, feeling pissed now. The three girls were all about nineteen or twenty. Dan had seen each of them in the office at one time or another.

'Your shout,' said Andrew, so Dan went back to the bar and returned with a jug. He surrendered to drunkenness and let it take him to a place where everything he heard was amusing and everything he said was funny and the girls were laughing along with him. Graham leant over and asked him, quietly, if he wanted to come back to his house with them and the girls, but Dan put his hand up in apologetic refusal and shook his head. He kept drinking and then he was outside with Graham, sharing a rollie, enjoying the unfamiliar taste of tobacco, and Graham was even more drunk than he was, trying to tell him he should stop being a 'floater' and 'commit' to the town.

'You'll be happier when you do,' said Graham, staggering slightly as he flicked the butt onto the street.

Back inside the hotel, Dan waited for Cassie to return but she didn't. Just before midnight, Andrew and Graham left with the three girls, walking in a ragged row abreast the road, towards Graham's house. Dan watched them go. He couldn't do it. He couldn't spy on Graham.

Alone now, he pushed himself away from the side of the hotel and began walking back towards the dump, towards home. He took a detour past the Rotary Park, its playground of derelict farm machinery made weird by the booze and the night, and then past Cassie's house.

Her lights were off. It was quiet. He hoped she was in bed, by herself. From here, the slag heap rising up behind him, he could see to the margins of town, where the blackness began, the lights of a road train breaching the hill on the town's southern edge. Beyond it, and on all sides, were hundreds of thousands of square kilometres of clapped-out mulga.

But Graham was right. There was a life to be lived here. Right here. It wasn't the edge of the world. That was somewhere further east or north, perhaps out near Fowler's station, he wasn't sure.

The Smell of Touch

How had he become so goddamn old? William Moore lowered himself down the steps at the front of his house. Where the hell was Maggie, and what was he doing out here anyway? He squinted across the road. He could make out the dark pines of the war memorial park opposite and, beyond that, the postcard blue of the Southern Ocean. Ah, that's right. The soap girl. Where was she?

Soap was one of their few indulgences. They lived a quiet life, listening to Radio National in the mornings, taking lunch under the grape-laden pergola in their backyard, a walk in the late afternoon on the headland. Below, the ocean, swelling incessantly.

Laura, the twenty-something granddaughter of one of Maggie's friends, had been supplying them with soap for the last three years. She and her husband, a tall, wiry man with hair that lay flat against his back in large knotted clumps, had a small property on the outskirts of town where they grew vegetables, kept chooks and made soap. Once a fortnight, Laura would do the rounds on her bike, stopping off at William and Maggie's house with a bar of soap and a carton of eggs. A quick chat and she'd be gone, onto her next customer.

Maggie was probably with Laura's grandmother right now.

*

'If I hit that leaf it means I've saved us from the Japs,' said Maggie to Billy as she lay prone on the dirt in his backyard, sighting along the barrel of her Daisy rifle through a gap in his mother's rosemary hedge.

Billy Moore kept his eye on the leaf – the tiny one sticking out by itself near the base of the oleander. The one he'd just missed. His mum was always telling him to stay away from that bush, and about the stockman who'd stirred his soup with an oleander branch and died a terrible, purple-faced death.

Maggie's leg pressed against Billy's. Eleven years old and she was already a crack shot. She held her breath and

Billy heard the click and faint schoock of the air-powered gun as the leaf oscillated briefly and then was still, now with a tiny hole in its centre. Maggie looked at him and grinned.

It was 1942. At the top of Spencer Gulf, locked by sea on one side and the desert on the other stood Port Augusta, a town of six thousand. Its children roamed the streets at will, their parents huddled around radios three times a day to listen to the news. They seemed to talk of little else but The Hun and The Nip Bastards, especially since the fall of Singapore. Maggie had an image in her mind of a race of small, yellow, dark-haired men, all exactly the same, massing to the north.

The two children had spent much of the summer in backyards and vacant lots, shooting The Hun on some dusty road in France or doing the same to The Nips in the viny, snake-infested jungles of New Guinea.

Maggie rolled away from Billy, spat a rosemary needle out of her mouth and sat in the dirt, the gun pointing over her shoulder to the blue.

'Okay,' conceded Billy. 'You win. What now?'

Maggie shrugged her shoulders. 'Dunno. What about lemons?'

Every house on the hill had a lemon tree but Billy knew she meant the one belonging to old Mrs Patterson and her ugly daughter, Gertrude. That tree sat in the middle of the Patterson's backyard, in full view of their kitchen window, but with enough cover on either side – the brick toilet block, a water tank, an untidy clump of hibiscus – to make stealing them a delicious possibility.

Billy grinned. 'Why not.'

*

When Constable Johnston had finished all his paperwork he scrubbed the floor of the cell with water and carbolic soap, the image of O'Reilly, on all fours, still working its unwanted way into his mind after all these months. He'd had to hit the lawyer twice to the side of his head to get him off the girl. He locked up and set off for home.

Over the bridge and up the hill to his little cottage with its view of the mangrove-bound port. Maggie, his niece, would be somewhere close, playing with Billy from across the road. O'Reilly would probably be in his backyard, pissing on his lemon tree. Johnston lengthened his stride.

Quickly up the steps to his veranda, he knocked the dust off his boots. No Sunshine. Something was wrong.

He opened the screen door and moved quickly through the house, glancing into each of the four rooms that came off the central hallway. Then into the back room and he could hear Sunshine whining now, and out into the backyard, Archie on the ground, eyes closed, his heavy chair with its metal axle overturned on the ground beside him.

'Archie,' he said and crouched down beside his brother.

'I'm okay,' said Archie and opened his eyes and Johnston could see they were shot with blood, brimming with tears. 'Just having a rest, mate.'

Johnston righted the wheelchair. Sunshine dropped slowly to his belly and edged forward, nuzzling Archie. 'I was just about to get up and make myself a cuppa,' said Archie. Johnston shooed Sunshine away, clutched his brother under his armpits and lifted him slowly into his chair.

William and Maggie arrived in Darwin in December 1965, in the crazy time between the Build Up and The Wet. The skies were black with massive anvil-clouds and the air sparked and fizzed with lightning. South Australia was another country and it quickly faded from their thoughts as they established themselves in Darwin society.

They were invited to parties overlooking the harbour and in the leafy, hilly parts of Ludmilla, in houses with plantation shutters and floors polished until you could see your face in them. The places where the doctors, lawyers, judges, newspaper proprietors, pearl dealers and other captains of commerce lived, and where the men all introduced themselves by surname first, conscious of their defining roles in the drama of this odd little city, closer to Jakarta than to Brisbane.

The city's only veterinarians, William and Maggie worked hard, treating everything from cats to crocodiles. When William was offered a government contract to control camp dogs in Aboriginal communities in the western Northern Territory, he jumped at the chance. Once a month, they would fly in to visit these remote cattle station and mission communities. From the air their shacks appeared as twenty or thirty tiny rectangles of iron amid vast expanses of black-soil plain and Mitchell Grass.

When the locals saw that William wasn't there to shoot all their dogs on sight, they welcomed the young couple. They set up clinics and injected the dogs with vitamins and antibiotics to treat their mange and scabies. The dogs became healthier and, with them, the Aboriginal children they lived alongside.

With their four weeks' holiday each year, William and Maggie made for the most remote parts of the western Northern Territory, revelling in its vastness and space. They explored the West Baines River to its source in the craggy limestone scree of Mt Behn, the

Tanami Desert, the natural galleries of Aboriginal art that ran for mile after mile beneath the overhang of the Newcastle Range.

Once William caught a barramundi so large that when it struck he thought he'd hooked a freshwater crocodile. That evening they took it back to Amanbidji and shared the feast with the traditional owners of the vast floodplain stretching to the west and north. On the ground outside a hut that was a jumble of cast-off pieces of iron and timber they played cards well into the evening.

On another trip William and Maggie were called on to treat a young Aboriginal man with sutures and antibiotics after he'd been speared in the thigh as payback for running over his nephew one moon-less night.

*

These things burned brightly for William. Massive suns of memory, their light travelling undaunted through the darkness to reach him. What happened yesterday, last month, last year, were meteoric flashes in comparison, burning themselves out in an instant.

William shuffled down the path to the letterbox and lifted the lid. No mail. He studied the sign beside their rosemary hedge. *House for sale.* Their house. Their home. They would have to leave their home? But he'd known that, hadn't he? Of course. They'd go back to Adelaide to live, where they'd be closer to ... closer to something or someone, he wasn't sure.

How had he become so goddamn old? Above him, a Black-shouldered Kite wheeled in the blue and another memory flooded his mind.

At the end of one of their holidays they had given two old Aboriginal women, sisters, a lift from Amanbidji to Yarralin. When they reached the tiny community, on the edge of the massive Victoria River Downs Station, they helped the old women out with their swags and pannikins. A young man ambled over from the nearest house to help. Mary, one of the sisters, clasped his face with her thin black fingers and wailed. He was from Mistake Creek and she hadn't seen him since he was a boy. He picked up her swag and swung it easily onto his broad shoulders and walked over to the sisters' house.

'Oh, poor bugger,' said Mary to her sister. 'Look at him.'

'Poor bugger,' said her sister, softly.

William and Maggie had heard this before. It was often how older Aboriginal women spoke on seeing young men and women they'd known only as children. Those who'd grown up since the last time they'd seen them. But why 'poor bugger'? The man was in the prime of his life. William and Mary had puzzled over it on their way back to Darwin.

*

Maggie and Billy dumped all bar two of the stolen lemons into an old crate on Billy's back veranda, covered them up with newspaper and kept going, into town, just in case the old bag had seen them and had a mind to visit and make trouble.

On the other side of the inlet they slid halfway down the embankment and scrambled around until they were underneath the bridge, its maze of thick timbers and blackened iron directly above them. This was a beaut place. Below them and twenty yards away, at the bottom of the embankment, sat the dark water. They could steal away from adults and lose themselves here in daydreams and the smell of mud.

Billy yanked his lemon out of one of his pockets, his pocket knife from the other. He opened the blade and sliced the fruit into rough quarters. He gave one to Maggie and they took turns pulling faces at each other as they sucked. Even stolen, it was tart. 'What'll happen to you and your dad?' asked Billy, in between grimaces.

'What do you mean?'

'You know. If your uncle has to go away to the war,' he said, licking the juice carefully off the blade of his knife and wiping it dry on his shorts. 'I mean, who'll look after you?'

Maggie studied a graze on her knee. She squeezed the lemon and the juice dripped and bit into the wound.

'He won't go away,' said Maggie, sounding braver than she was, and tossed the shuddery lemon into the water and picked up her rifle. 'Let's go,' she said, and ran down the embankment towards the water, veering away from its edge as she ran.

Billy caught up with her after a while and she slowed down to a walk as they entered the main street of Port Augusta. From the wharves they could hear the sound of men hitting things with hammers.

'My turn with the gun,' said Billy, and Maggie walked another obstinate twenty paces before unshouldering the rifle and passing it to him.

Past the post office they walked, the school behind looming as an ironclad reminder that this was Sunday, and Sunday afternoon at that. Maggie tried not to think of her teacher, Mrs O'Reilly.

*

Later, Maggie lay in the grass at the end of her backyard, half hidden by a clump of rosemary at the edge of O'Reilly's patch of lawn, ten feet from the lawyer's lemon tree. 'The Ambidexter' as her father and uncle called him. She didn't know what it meant, but it didn't sound good, at least not the way her uncle said it. She knew something bad had happened. Her *father and uncle sometimes stopped talking when she entered a room.*

The evening was warm and she lay there, tired of imagining enemies. O'Reilly's axe sat wedged into the chopping block by his back door, its handle pointing stiffly at her.

It startled her when he emerged from his house, striding towards the tree.

When O'Reilly's step faltered, Maggie knew he'd seen her, but he kept on, stopped by the tree, unzipped himself and stood there, urinating. Maggie kept her eyes on the ground until she could no longer hear the tinkle of piss, but when she looked up he hadn't moved and she saw his cock half hidden by the darkness between his legs and she turned away, rolled over and ran back through the yard.

*

And now, at last, William understood. The old women were sad *for* the young, whose lives were spiralling out behind them – the gyrations of character, personality and missed opportunity growing ever wider

– without them even knowing it. Just as their own lives had done. That man-child at Yarralin, in his mid twenties but already with one foot in the grave, hurtling towards old age. 'Poor bugger.'

'Yes!' he said. He felt a rush like he'd solved one of the mysteries of life. He *must* tell Maggie when she got back from her farewells.

'Hello William.'

Startled, he turned. It was Laura, the soap girl. Her pale prettiness was disarranged by the bucket hat she wore in place of a helmet.

'Hello Laura,' he said. 'What have you got for us?'

She leant her bike against the fence and stumbled slightly as she did so, half-falling against it. William shuffled forward, as fast as he could. Laura grunted as the bike slid underneath her and then she was on her backside on the footpath.

'Oh, my dear!' said William, reaching down to her, one hand on the fence. She gave a faint smile, took his hand and slowly stood up.

William helped her right the bike. Cakes of soap, each one wrapped in tissue paper, had spilled from her front carrier. Ten cartons of eggs, held in place on the rear carrier with ocky straps, had barely moved, but the ends of some of them had staved in and were already leaking yolk and white.

Inside the house, William gave her a glass of cold water and she sat in the dining room, drinking slowly, her arms resting on the cool jarrah table. It was a beautiful room. A bay window held a view of the memorial pines, framed by leadlight parrots. An upright piano, open. Landscapes in watercolours on the walls.

She had never been inside before. It was a house that held the presence, in the scent and tone of its air, of thirty-thousand-odd days of detritus and use, of forgotten visitors, long-gone pets, accidents, joys, sickness, celebration and grief.

She gave the old man a smile. 'I'm pregnant,' she said. 'Five months to go. Can't keep a thing down.'

Poor bugger, thought William. He offered her toast, then some fruit, but she wouldn't take either, so he gave her twenty dollars for the soap and a carton of eggs and refused to take the change. He saw her off with a wave from his veranda. *Billy knew he was in trouble as soon as he saw the look on Mrs O'Reilly's face. The older kids called her 'The Snapdragon'. He walked around the corner of the timber-framed schoolhouse and there she was, a look of fury on her face. Billy wondered for a second if he should run, but then it was too late. She was on him, her hand on his shoulder, nails digging into his skin.*

'You little bugger,' she said, her mouth twitching with anger. She marched him into the classroom and made him sit on the floor underneath her table while the others had lunch.

Maggie poked her head around the open doorway but Mrs O'Reilly saw her, picked up the duster on her table and threw it at her. Maggie ducked and ran back to the yard.

'I expect you know what I'm going to do to you,' said Mrs O'Reilly.

Billy stayed silent. He knew exactly what she'd do. 'O'Reilly fucked a half-caste girl,' he'd told his classmates at morning recess as they sat on the hard boughs of the old pepper tree on the edge of the school grounds. He wasn't even sure what it meant, but he knew it was wrong. One of the younger kids must've overheard him and told Mrs O'Reilly.

After the bell had rung and all the children returned to class, Mrs O'Reilly gave Maggie an empty tin and told her to fill it up with water. Billy sat despondently underneath Mrs O'Reilly's desk. Her lace-up shoes were the ugliest he'd ever seen on a woman.

When Maggie returned with the tin of water, Mrs O'Reilly stood up from her chair and walked silently to the back of the room where she kept a bar of soap for just such an occasion. The class was silent. No one turned to watch her as she picked up the soap and walked back to her desk and dropped it in the water. She reached down, grabbed a handful of Billy, and hauled him out.

'Right,' she said. 'This is what happens when a child in my class uses foul language. Open your mouth.'

Billy hesitated and she dug her fingers into his hair and pulled so that his face was raised to her. She scooped out the soap and rammed it between his lips and yanked his hair again so that he cried out and the soap slid between his teeth. She worked it around Billy's mouth while he spluttered and gagged. 'There,' she said, releasing his hair, her face red and ugly. 'Anyone else with a foul mouth that needs washing?'

No one looked at her.

*

Late afternoon. Maggie lay prone on the ground at the end of her yard, waiting for the enemy, loading and firing her Daisy rifle. Shot after shot, each one deadly accurate. Within ten minutes she'd deposited a tiny slug of lead into each of the lemons on O'Reilly's tree.

The screen door banged open and O'Reilly sauntered out into the yard, making for the lemon tree. He unzipped and stood there, his cock snaking out of its dark nest. Maggie kept her eye on him this time, aiming the rifle carefully. As a stream of urine splattered onto the dry ground, O'Reilly noticed something odd about the lemon in front of his face. He kept pissing as he looked at its neighbour and then another and another and saw that each fruit had been sabotaged.

'Bloody hell,' he said, and Maggie gently squeezed the trigger and the pellet hit him on the end of his cock and he screamed and fell to his knees.

*

Later, when Maggie called out sweetly from the front door and his heart lurched as it always did, William remembered vaguely he had something to tell her, but couldn't remember what. They had afternoon tea together in the dining room and he opened the carefully wrapped bar of soap and smelled rosemary and he was back, alongside Maggie, shooting things with her Daisy rifle, his leg pressed against hers.

The Gap Between the Sandbars

Tuesday, 2 September

A fine drizzle pricks my face as I lob an off-cut of treated pine at the cat that woke me up. The ginger Tom ducks over our eastern fence, followed by the poisonous lump of pine, and I wince as an image of the eco-warrior who lives next door floods my groggy, pre-dawn mind.

I'm in the front yard of our Largs Bay home. A mild nervous breakdown sees me, for the first time in a long time, fit for nothing much but taxiing my children from home to school and back again. The sun will rise soon.

I'm on extended leave from my ten-year stint in middle management in the Department of Premier and Cabinet. The so-called Communications unit. On one level it's a relief to be out of there, if only for a couple of months. I was sure I was going to kill someone.

Three hundred metres to the west lies the murky waters of Gulf St Vincent, the massive body of water and tidal flats wedged between Yorke Peninsula and the Adelaide plains. In two or three hundred years, this'll all be underwater. We're on borrowed time. Above, the power cables moan with the wind off the gulf. Across the road, the Jacksons' white picket fence glows in the milky light, a constant reproach.

*

Jack and Sarah are in the back of the car. Twins. I read somewhere that twins are more commonplace than we think, at least in the womb. But something will often go wrong, one of the embryos will fail and then will be 'swallowed up' by the other, leaving no trace of its existence. This may explain some of the natural antagonism these two display. I can imagine them eyeing each other off *in utero,* watching each other for the first sign of failure.

We're off to school. The car is barely out of the driveway before Sarah starts up.

'Which is better, Jack? A tiny piece of ice or a tiny piece of snow?'

I look at her ten-year-old face in the rear-view mirror, bright with feigned innocence.

'Ah, ice. No, snow. No, ice!' says Jack, panic in his voice by the time he gets to the third option.

'Which one?' asks Sarah, all sweetness and light.

His voice drops. 'Ice. A tiny piece of ice.' The panic has gone, replaced with resignation. He knows he's going to fall into a trap no matter what his answer is. He just wants it over and done with. I'm with him on that.

'Well, they're the same thing. Ice and snow are the same.'

'No they're not.'

'Yes they are.'

'DAD!' he yells.

Parenthood has been a confusion of delights and devastations. One morning they're at me, mercilessly pushing all my buttons, undoing my defences one by one just to see how they work, messing with my mind. The next they beg me 'Do the rubbish truck, Daddy!' and they lie side by side on the lounge-room floor, covered in rugs as I rumble around, gears screeching. I pick up each one in turn, hoist them over my shoulder and 'dump' them on the lounge as they giggle and squeal.

What is *that* all about? Wanting to trust someone else? Or wanting confirmation that someone close to you is powerful beyond your comprehension? That would be a comfort I guess. A comfort that adulthood will strip from them as quickly and cleanly as scales from a freshly caught fish.

Part of the deal to keep my job is regular meetings with a counsellor. Bruce is a local man: a decade or so older than me, a drinker, with a degree in philosophy and unorthodox methods. Narrative therapy. I'm to write things down. Find a way to understand my life as an unfolding story.

He thinks I should seize the chance and opt out for a year or two. Renovate myself (not the house), grow tomatoes, help out occasionally at the school canteen. Middle-manage my waistline. *Get back to basics.* He's an unreconstructed hippy. We have a session each week, paid for by the department.

*

But the first thing on my list this morning is the white picket fence. Thirteen months ago, our entire fence fell over one windy August night. The idiots-we-bought-this-house-from used untreated pine for all their outdoor projects. Saved themselves a couple of bucks, put up a facade, and sold the problem on to us. The posts were riddled with white ants.

I'm glad to be outside. The shower is dripping. You can hear it from any room in the house. I've changed the washer, to no avail. That steady *drip drip drip* makes me feel less of a man. I'm taking things way too seriously.

I set to work. Yesterday I put in the posts, sawing timber, digging holes, mixing concrete. I spent an anxious twenty minutes aligning each one as the concrete set around them. I was a mess by the time I'd finished. Hands raw and tight from cement dust. Hamstrings ablaze.

The posts look fine. Now I have to cut notches for the horizontals to rest in. I have no idea how to do this properly. And it's clear to me that for every possible task there's at least a million dumb ways of doing it and two or three really clever and elegant ones.

As I'm pondering the problem, Ken, the retired naval engineer from two doors down, shuffles by and asks if I need a hand. He tells me to use a circular saw to make horizontal cuts in the posts and then a chisel to knock out the waste. Sounds good. He offers me his saw. Within minutes we've clamped one of the cross-struts to the poles and I've marked out exactly where the cuts will go.

We toddle off to his house to get the saw. It's a Californian bungalow, circa 1920, with honeysuckle covering the front veranda. Ken's wife of forty-five years died ten months ago and a group of us have been looking out for him. It's that kind of street. A small, leafy oasis of friendliness, three streets back from the gulf.

'How are you, Alan?' he asks, as he puts a cup of tea in front of me on the kitchen table. Ken's hair has gone a bit wild and he's wearing a brown cardigan and trousers. You rarely see him in anything else. Besides that, he's holding up reasonably well.

'Ah, you know. Doing okay.' I take a sip of hot, sweet tea. 'I've got the team-building thing on Thursday. We'll see how it goes.'

Wednesday, 3 September

When I pick up the kids from school, I notice Jack has a smug little smile on his face. *Here we go.* He waits until we're in the car.

'Which is better?' he offers Sarah. 'A telescope or nothing?'

He's obviously put a lot of thought into this. A lot of thought for a ten-year-old boy, that is.

'Nothing,' snaps Sarah.

'Why, Sarah? You can see things from a long way with a telescope.'

'Nothing.'

'Don't you want to be able to do that?' says Jack.

'No.'

Silence.

I half-remember a quote from my university days – American Literature 210. Something along the lines that a man – a real man, that is – could be destroyed but not defeated. Judging by the look on his face, Jack's got quite a few years to go.

*

After dinner, I read a carpentry book while Donna is on the phone to her mum, my mind wandering to tomorrow. The team-building workshop was another thing I agreed to so I could keep my job. As I'm thinking about it I feel the first prickle of panic and I try to empty my mind but, too late, the prickles multiply and take over.

It's like when I go for a swim in the gulf on a warm summer's night. I walk out to the gap between the first and second sandbars. Then, in waist-deep water, I begin swimming, parallel to the shore, the vast expanse of the gulf on my left. The seabed shelves away into the deep, where the sharks live. We have big ones here – Great Whites, five metres long. Fish that can bite you in half. The seabed shelves away ... but

I don't look or else I'll lose my nerve and stop swimming.

I'll have to take a pill to get to sleep now.

What is the problem? Why the breakdown? I haven't figured it out yet. Clearly it has a lot to do with the feeling I had in Premier and Cabinet that I was achieving nothing of real importance in my work, engineering the re-election of a politician I had lost all respect for.

And then there was Shaun. My boss. A 'whizz-kid' at communications, he had very quickly cottoned on to one of the guiding principles of advancement in the public service – appropriate the work of those below you in the food chain and pass it off as your own.

I know that I grew to hate my workplace. I developed a rash that, at one point, engulfed my entire body. I stopped sleeping. I felt weak but couldn't find a way forward. My head felt as if it had been hollowed out and pumped full of gas. I had to get out.

Thursday, 4 September

I find myself sitting on a bare wooden floor in a renovated church in Unley. It's cold. Around me sit my workmates, each with a pillow, each of us concentrating on our breathing as Julia, our twenty-something, yoga-teaching, tofu-eating 'work relations consultant' circles us, critiquing our collective lack of posture and our total inability to breath as nature intended.

Ours is the most dysfunctional unit within Premier and Cabinet. It's no surprise that we are the first group chosen to undergo a team-building workshop. We're the guinea pigs and it's clear, right away, that the 'facilitators' are new to this and gloriously out of their depth.

Somewhere during the morning session – between having to pretend that our bodies are trees swaying in the wind and watching Samantha, our Communications Officer, silently pour a cup of cold water over Shaun's head – Cecilia, the thirty-something project officer I got on with best, sidles up to me with a question.

'Did you ever have moments when you thought, "If I wasn't here, would I be missed"?'

'All the time,' I said, and we both laughed out loud.

But it was the exercise in which we were made to sit in a circle and each say something positive about a nominated person that drove Samantha to do what she did with the cup of water.

Friday, 5 September

I spend the morning outdoors helping Ken with his paving, glad to be doing something that will result in soreness and tiredness and allow me to surrender to sleep.

At 3.20 I pick up the kids from school. There's something on Sarah's mind.

'We're not gonna leave, are we?'

'What do you mean?' I ask, looking at her in the mirror.

'I heard you and mummy talking about the house.'

I remember the conversation. The what-happens-if-I-can't-go-back-to-work chat. The how-will-we-pay-the-mortgage chat. Donna, bless her, assured me we'd get by. We'd just have to cut back, maybe get some chooks and plant more veggies, maybe I could bone up on the renovation stuff and set myself up as an odd-job man for a while. Paving, carpentry, fencing, gardening. Plenty of work around.

'Don't worry, honey,' I tell Sarah. 'We're not going anywhere.'

After I've dropped them off at Nanna's I continue into the city, looking for a sign. Should I go back to work?

When I walk into the building I came to loathe, the first person I see is Shaun, at the downstairs cafe. Neither of us wants this but he indicates the chair opposite him and I sit down. He's drinking a coffee, his eyes darting constantly to his watch. He asks me how my leave is going and I tell him about the paving.

'And you're happy?' he asks after a while, as if he can't imagine it is possible.

'Yeah, I am.' I look down at my hands and my nails are blackened and I have the beginnings of calluses on my palms. I notice him looking at them.

'All my own work,' I say to Shaun, and smile. He doesn't even blush. There it is, I think to myself. There it is.

Landscapes

Late afternoon. Vanessa stood outside the most expensive real estate money could buy in Victor Harbor and smiled for the first time that day. She expected to make $60000 from this sale. There was a Jeffrey Smart painting – leaden sky, yellow street sign – coming up for auction next week in Adelaide. She wanted it.

The house was new – four hundred square metres of marbled floor on two levels. Its facade alternated thick plastered walls with expanses of smoked glass. Vanessa knew the owner had baulked in the final stages. Overwhelmed by the cost and by his losses on the stock market, he had insisted the builder not use the double-glazed glass the plans prescribed. So it would cost a fortune to keep cool in summer and warm in winter.

With a property like this, the trick was not to talk too much, just allow the grandeur of the view to do its work, without interruption. The client would walk up the central staircase and into the upstairs living room and be faced immediately with floor-to-ceiling glass, framing a seascape beyond reproach. She looked at her watch.

*

'Permanent, infinite views,' she said to the young man with a blonde on either arm. He let out a low whistle of approval. He sized up the room, replete with all the props a house like this demanded – black leather couches, an expensive globe of the world on a mahogany stand by the glass wall. And there it was – the telescope on the balcony.

'Claudia, look. Look at that,' he said. Vanessa heard the little catch in his voice as he realised that this, right here, was the life he'd been promised in all the lifestyle porn he'd flicked through every Sunday morning over Florentine eggs and a double macchiato in Hindley Street.

One of the girls – Vanessa was sure they were sisters – unhooked herself from the man and sauntered over to the window. She draped herself across a black leather chair, her mini-skirt riding up the half-inch required to remove all doubt from the mind of a man. Her red knickers, Vanessa judged, were an almost perfect colour match for the low-slung car they'd pulled up in.

'We'll take it,' she said, and the young man laughed rich and loud. Vanessa found it hard to take her eyes off him. There was a swagger in his every move. The intoxication of knowing that you could buy anything you looked at.

'And what would we do down here during the week?' said the other blonde. She looked a year or two older. Her skirt rode an inch or two lower.

'Everything you've always wanted,' said the young man, taking her hand and steering her towards the view of the bay.

As they took it all in, Vanessa said nothing of the bikies, the casual lawlessness of the summer crowd, the recent downturn in sales. 'Buyer beware,' was her motto, and she knew they'd give as good as they got. All-night parties, young things wearing five-hundred-dollar tracksuits, cocktails of drugs. The soundtrack to their lives would be all synthetic drums and bass, bereft of melody, at 120 decibels. There would be complaints.

*

By contrast, the house on Bennett Street in Goolwa wasn't much to look at. Bright blue weatherboard with white trim around the windows, doors and gutters, it was a fisherman's shack masquerading as a Greek Island villa. Surrounded by fresh McMansions, it stood smack in the middle of an unfenced, treeless nine-hundred-square-metre block. *Try buying one of those now for less than a million,* thought Vanessa, as she walked up the steps.

Vanessa had grown up on one of the more prestigious properties in the district – an 1870s homestead on 180 acres of land to the north-west of Victor Harbor, with views of Granite Island. When her father died five years ago, she was thirty and forced to move. The cafe she managed had failed and she had gone to work as a personal assistant to a real estate agent. There had been many things he had asked her to attend to until, finally, she had married him.

She banged on the screen door, brushing a piece of lint off her charcoal-grey jacket.

'It's open, come in,' a voice called out.

Vanessa opened the mesh door and stepped into the little shack. This was hers. She liked to drop in once a fortnight to collect the rent and check on her investment and David didn't seem to mind. The living room opened up to her right. There was the same odour she always smelt and she saw the crayons, the cloudy jam jars bristling with brushes, and she was back in the crafts building at Victor Harbor High in her school uniform.

'David,' she called out. 'Vanessa. Here for the rent.'

*

David had moved to Goolwa when Adelaide became unbearable. With a modest inheritance from his mother he left his public service job and vowed never to return. He was looking for somewhere to rest and paint, and to ponder how he'd ended up, at the age of thirty-three, without a partner and with a job he couldn't care less about.

He had stayed a night in a motel on the outskirts of Goolwa and walked the two kilometres into town the next morning, along dusty, narrow roads bereft of footpaths. He had seen right away it was a town living within its means, where things that weren't absolutely necessary to keep the wheels of commerce turning just weren't built. It was also a lot flatter than he'd remembered, and a lot less interesting, landscape-wise.

Behind the locked-up public toilets he tucked his shirt into his jeans and then presented himself to the real estate office. He filled out a form while the receptionist smiled to herself and joked on the phone. Then he was ushered into Vanessa's office – all brown leather and pine furniture stained to resemble walnut. It was during the interview with her that David realised how horribly lonely he was. His eyes kept lodging within Vanessa's cleavage and his head swam with her scent.

Now, thirteen months later, he felt as if he was just beginning to paint the way he always knew he could.

*

Vanessa could see him through the open sliding doors dividing the living room from the kitchen. Around her were dozens of large sketches, on the walls and on the bare wooden floorboards, mainly landscapes. A couple were rendered in charcoal and pencil in broad, fluid strokes that reminded her of a Brett Whiteley her father had owned. The others were fine-grained studies in watercolour and ink.

A portrait caught her attention. Vanessa raised an eyebrow and stopped breathing for a second or two. 'Tea,' she called out distractedly to David's question as he clattered around the kitchen.

The subject of the portrait was a woman of indeterminate age with a slight tummy. She was sitting on a kitchen table, her body square on to the viewer but with knees demurely together. Wearing a grey jacket, undone, her left breast exposed and the nipple aroused. The woman's hair was black, cut into a bob, curling up onto her face on the right. It was herself, unmistakeably.

'I thought you did landscapes,' she called out at last.

'I do,' came the voice from the kitchen.

'So what's this then? Time out?'

David walked into the living room, avoiding her gaze. He moved to the table in the centre of the room and began straightening it, putting brushes into pots, a litter of crayons into a biscuit tin, a faint blush on his cheek.

'Or is this a new type of landscape?' she suggested, gesturing at the portrait. His hunched shoulders emboldened her. 'The secret geography of the body, perhaps.'

She waited for him to answer, half expecting him to talk of the body as a landscape, perhaps something lyrical of mountains, valleys, denuded hills, unexpected lush hollows.

'I'll get the rent,' he said, and disappeared back into the kitchen. She could hear him opening a drawer, rummaging through it.

Her phone rang and when she looked at the screen she knew she'd be hanging that Jeffrey Smart in her living room within a week. She let it go through to message bank. Apart from the table and the clutter of art, the room she was in was bare but for a two-seater lounge in a drab purple fabric and a knotty pine coffee table that spoke of Centrelink and debt. David was almost her age and yet, looking around, she knew she could buy his life a dozen times over.

Vanessa reached into her purse, pulled out three fresh fifty-dollar notes and put them on the table. She picked up her portrait and walked through the room, into the hallway, and out to her car under a sky daubed with colour.

The Dress

I

Ruth Anderson stood before her dresser mirror and cast a critical eye over her reflection. Dark hair; a squareness to her face that suggested hardness; still slim-waisted at thirty-four. From outside came the thud and crack of wood being chopped in the yard below. She moved to the window and watched as Harold, her husband, sundered a piece of red gum. *To be reduced to this!* she thought. *Niggers' work.*

From her upstairs bedroom in the Royal Mail Hotel, Ruth could see the mangrove-lined port. In the distance, pale blue as if all the earth's colour had been sucked dry by heat, the Flinders Range. Nearer, on a vacant half-acre of dirt and low scrub, crisscrossed by trails running from the harbour to the hotel and back, Grace Williams was returning from the butcher's. *Thank God for Grace,* thought Ruth. *Without her to help...* Port Augusta had lost many of its men and women to the armed forces and the munitions factories in Adelaide. Ruth turned away from the window.

Downstairs, Harold leant on his axe, a sheen of brandied sweat covering his bare torso, and stole a glance at Grace in her faded hibiscus dress as she walked across the hotel yard, carrying a parcel of meat.

'Morning missy,' he said. Thin lips split his face into a straight, hard line. A mouth like a vice. Once or twice, within the darkness of the hotel hallway, he'd caught sight of her on the back doorstep, the light streaming through that thin dress, making it all but transparent against her dusky skin. Each time the image stayed with him for days.

'Morning, Mr Anderson.' Grace nodded and walked quickly past him. She put the parcel into the meat-safe, then went to the washhouse. She set to work, building a fire to heat the water. The smell of burning eucalypt took her back to the mission on the outskirts of town where she'd grown up. During her mother's last days at the mission Grace had done all their washing in a kerosene tin over an open fire.

On the staircase, on her way to strip the beds, Grace paused to listen. She could hear Harold in the front bar now, stacking glasses. She had been wary of him ever since he'd cornered her once on the upstairs landing and backed her against the wall, his meaty hand on her belly, his thick sausage fingers angling down. As she began stripping the first of the upstairs rooms, she kept an ear out for him.

*

Mid morning and heat had cleared the streets. On her way back from the post office, Ruth walked past the stone-walled grounds of the church. A poster advertised the upcoming gala concert – a fundraiser for the troops overseas. One bright thing amid the dreariness of wartime Port Augusta. For Ruth it was as if the people left here – the shop owners, railmen, clerks, the aged, mad and ill – had been left to their own devices. Forgotten about.

Ruth's father had once all but owned this town – several hotels, the bakery, the iceworks and nearly a dozen properties. Ruth's mother had been active in the church and on every committee that mattered. She had raised her children up to believe in God, in the sanctity of property, and in the self-evident truth that there was no such thing as the deserving poor; that behind every family down on their luck was a character study of profligacy, dullness or apathy.

But the Great Depression had stripped away more than half of the family's fortune and they had abandoned the town in 1931, retreating to the eastern suburbs of Adelaide. Only Ruth had stayed, marrying Harold, her father's ex-accountant.

All they had at the moment was the lease on the Royal Mail Hotel and two hundred pounds in the bank in Adelaide. She dreamt of the day she'd own the hotel, become a matriarch of this little town and undo what had been done.

*

Back inside the Royal Mail, Ruth drew the blinds against the sun and sat down in the dining room with a cup of tea. Grace had already cleared away the remains of breakfast but, Ruth noticed, had yet to sweep the floor.

A hesitant knock sounded on the dining-room door and a woman, dressed in overalls, edged into the room. Anne Hargreaves.

'Are we still on for this morning?' asked Anne.

The way the woman tried to round her vowels irritated Ruth to the point of distraction. But she steadied herself.

'Of course,' she said, standing and picking up her half-finished drink. What choice did she have? When Anne had approached her the previous week for the use of her dining room for her camouflage-net-making group, Ruth had searched for a reason to deny her, but it was useless. Anne's work was for the war effort. And the past was the past, wasn't it?

Anne walked into the room, followed by her little group of earnest women. Half a dozen of them, the wives of doctors, businessmen and bankers, they affected the clothing of the Women's Land Army – overalls over plain, long-sleeved shirts. Some of them had never before set foot inside the Royal Mail and they came in quietly, perhaps mindful of history and gossip.

The last two women carried nets and tools stretchered on a piece of canvas. Ruth leant out into the hallway and hollered 'Grace', and the girl came at a good pace. While Ruth helped Anne and the women arrange themselves at tables, Grace made tea.

When the women began to busy themselves with their nets and needles, Ruth retreated to the front bar. The men had gone quiet at the sight of the silent procession of women. The travelling salesman, the sandalwood cutters, the puffed up alderman and the dentist were all staring into their beers, wishing themselves somewhere else, doing something useful for the war effort.

Ruth left Harold to run the bar and found refuge upstairs, dusting rooms that had not been let for several weeks. Occasionally she wandered downstairs and stuck her head inside the dining room to see how the women were going.

'We're all fine,' Anne would say, looking up from the net she was working on.

Later, Ruth ordered Grace into the kitchen to begin preparing lunch. When she came back into the dining room, the women had finished packing their equipment into the wooden crates Old Charlie Farquhar, the yardsman, had dragged in from the storeroom.

'Thank you so much,' said Anne. 'For your hospitality, and for making this room available.'

'Not at all,' said Ruth, surprised by the satisfaction blooming inside her. This was surely a conciliatory gesture on Anne's part and it would be churlish to not accept it.

*

The following morning, Anne was again effusive with her thanks. 'Why don't you join us?' she asked.

Pleased with the attention she was getting from the women, Ruth smiled but shook her head. 'I'm sorry. I have far too much work to do.' Then, partly to keep Anne in her place, she added, 'Perhaps I could let Grace do a little each day,' thinking that the woman would recognise the slight and say 'no'.

But she didn't.

'Thank you, Ruth,' Anne said. 'That would be lovely.'

*

Grace sat with Anne and Mrs Townsend, the bank manager's wife, as Anne showed her how to make a net. The Aboriginal girl quickly got the hang of it and Anne praised her dexterity.

'I heard that your people were good at this sort of thing,' she said. 'But I would never have believed *how good.*'

Grace kept working on the net, careful not to draw attention to herself.

Ruth bustled around with a dustpan and broom in the hallway, just within earshot. The women were largely oblivious to her presence now, talking excitedly about arrangements for the gala concert in two weeks' time and the dresses they had ordered from Adelaide. Anne was on the gala concert committee. She had been chosen to welcome and introduce the dignitaries and military brass from Adelaide.

'It's such an honour,' said Mrs Townsend, as Ruth came in to rattle knives and forks at the dining room dresser. Murmurs of agreement from among the women. Ruth glared across the room at Anne and Grace, then stomped out. Made to feel like a servant in her own hotel. *And by Anne Hargreaves.* What would her mother say?

*

Later that week, Ruth invited one of her mother's old friends, Mrs Patterson, for morning tea. This was the quiet time of the day for Ruth, in between the breakfast and lunch guests, and not many of either in these days of rations and decrees. From the doorway of the dining room came the front bar sounds of men hiding from the heat, glasses in hand.

Mrs Patterson had seen Anne Hargreaves talking to Miss Shadforth, the slender missionary, outside Taylor's Emporium. 'I don't trust those two,' she said. 'Hargreaves and that stick insect. They're as thick as thieves.' She coughed into her handkerchief. 'And we know who they're trying to steal, don't we?'

'Not if I can help it,' said Ruth, dabbing at her brow with a napkin.

'They probably think she's too good to work in a hotel,' said Mrs Patterson. The older woman had a knack for saying things like that. Things that were true but which hurt.

At the sound of voices coming from outside, Mrs Patterson stood up and went to the window. 'I think you should see this,' she said, not turning around.

Old Charlie and Grace were sitting side by side near the woodheap. Grace was laughing at something the old man had said, balancing her lunch – a plate of beans – on her lap.

Ruth got up from the dining table and walked over to where the older woman stood. She groaned at the sight. 'Right,' she said, striding out of the room.

Grace stopped eating, her fork in mid air, when Ruth burst out of the hotel. Mrs Patterson edged out onto the back step, taking it all in.

'What do you think you're doing?' Ruth said, her voice so husky and low with anger it was all she could do to force out a sound. 'How dare you!' She stopped, five yards away from the old man and the girl. 'How dare you eat on the woodheap like a station nigger! Get to your room this instant.'

Grace sat there.

'Go to your room and eat your meal!' squawked Ruth.

'I'm not hungry,' said Grace. She put down her plate, spilling beans on the ground. She didn't move.

Mrs Patterson's eyes bored into the back of Ruth's head, and Ruth knew the older woman was expecting her to crush the girl. 'You are forgetting yourself, miss,' Ruth said and stood there, wanting to sling Grace to the ground. Impossible. She turned away, bustling Mrs Patterson in front of her.

When she had gone, Grace picked up her plate and took it back to her room. Charlie kneeled on the ground, placing a shard of red gum on the fire beneath his billy. He remembered working at Erinlea Station; how the blackfellas there would eat their dinner on the woodheap at the back of the kitchen after having put in a long day's work, the equal of any white man. He had taken his meal out there to join them. They had sacked him after his fight with the foreman the next day. Had to really; he'd bitten off half the bastard's right ear. Still, he knew better than to interfere in the affairs of women.

*

On the morning of the sixth day of The Occupation, as Ruth had come to think of it, she told the women that she was sorry, but their presence was interfering too much with the running of the hotel. Ruth looked Anne directly in the eye when she said 'interfering too much' and held her gaze until Anne looked away.

II

Even after months of living rough with the blackfellas north of Ooldea, the heat was almost unbearable. Hot air blasted from a ragged hole in the engine well as Peter Dingo turned off the northern road and headed for the centre of town. As he passed the hospital he remembered his last day in town, three months ago. He had carried Grace's mother from the hospital, her kidneys useless, and propped her up with pillows in the cab of his truck. Before they reached the mission, she had put her hand on his arm and told him of the street in Port Adelaide where Grace could find her uncles, aunts and cousins.

'They wouldn't do this to a white woman,' he had said to the missionary-in-charge as he carried Mrs Williams into the mission's sickbay. Grace was at his elbow, fussing and distraught. Miss Shadforth had put a finger up to her pursed lips. Peter had looked right through her.

Peter Dingo pulled up outside the police station, climbed out and threw his hat on the seat. On the tray of the Whippet Buckboard lay two sets of scalps, threaded on fencing wire, writhing with flies. Each had a loop of wire at the end for a handle. He picked them up and walked to the station, swinging the scalps as he went.

Inside, Sergeant Armstrong sat at his desk at the back of the room, wiping the sweat from his face with a rag. Constable Johnston sat in one corner, typing a two-fingered report. Peter walked to the front counter dividing the room.

'Got something for you,' he said. He held up the scalps and smiled.

'Oh, for fuck's sake, Dingo,' said the Sergeant. 'Take 'em round the back.'

Peter laughed, then walked back into the hammering heat and down the laneway that separated the station from the Sergeant's residence. He laid the scalps near a listless lemon tree, unbuttoned himself and let out a yellow stream at the base. Constable Johnston emerged from the back of the station.

'Trying to finish it off?' he asked, jutting his chin at the tree.

Peter grunted and buttoned his pants.

'How many?' asked Johnston.

'Two hundred and sixty.'

Johnston gave a low whistle. 'You've done well.'

Peter grabbed hold of the makeshift handles, lifting the scalps off the ground. They flicked around his legs, sending up thick black clouds of flies.

His forearms danced with muscle and Johnston thought of the hawsers used to tie up the fishing boats in the harbour. You had to hand it to him, thought Johnston, the dogger earnt his money. Shoulder-length hair, torn trousers and a filthy shirt; covered in dust from heel to crown. Spending months at a time in marginal cattle country between Ooldea and Marree, trading with the natives for the scalps of the pups they ate as a delicacy in spring.

*

With close to a hundred and sixty pounds stowed away safely in his swag, Peter turned into Church Street and parked outside the Royal Mail. Four shillings a day bought him a room upstairs and the use of a tiny, windowless bathroom at the end of the hall. He gave a week's keep to Harold Anderson, then dragged himself up the stairs to a tub of tepid water that turned to madeira with dust by the time he had finished. His first proper bath for weeks.

In his room he changed into a fresh set of moleskin trousers and red serge shirt, combed his hair, unpacked his bags and sat for a minute on the narrow bed to take in the room. A wardrobe, one chair and a pockmarked, red cedar writing desk. A door opened onto the darkened first-floor balcony. He rolled up his dirty clothes and placed them neatly outside his door, in the hallway. He hadn't seen Grace yet. He hoped she was still here.

Downstairs, in the bar, Peter Dingo felt hemmed in by the low ceiling and strained joking of the men from the railyards and the iceworks as they talked of Hitler and Hirohito. When Harold Anderson began blustering about Spear Creek, Peter walked out and into the yard, clutching a bottle of beer. Old Charlie sat near the woodpile, a seven-ounce butcher in hand.

'Mind if I join ya?' Peter asked the old man.

'Free country,' said Charlie, motioning with a chin like a knob of cucumber at a log alongside him.

'For the time being it is.' The evening was still, the smell of mangrove heavy in the air. Behind them, the Flinders Range reared up like the last wave on earth. 'Still working then?' Peter asked the old man.

'Still working. Won't let me quit.' Charlie hawked up a load of phlegm and spat it neatly onto the ground beside him.

Peter looked at Charlie in his baggy grey trousers and red braces and saw himself in forty years' time if he stayed in the game. A bushman, a jack-of-all-trades, shuffling through his last days as a yardie, a hotel dogsbody. Charlie had been one of the best doggers in his day. Five-foot-five, skinny as a budgie in a storm. But by fuck he could fight if the stories were true.

'Thinkin' of getting a new truck,' said Peter.

'You wanna put some money away,' said Charlie. 'Buy yerself some property somewhere. A house in town you can rent, live in when you're too old to dog.'

'Still got a few years left in me,' said Peter. 'I'm doing alright.'

'That's what I used to say,' said Charlie. 'Look at me now. Nothin'. Just a swag.'

Charlie sat looking up at the darkness, remembering the brilliant, cold points of light and their names. A life lived under sky, his world bound only by the slow fall and curve of horizon. Hundreds of campsites across three states. Knew each one like the back of his hand. Each morning coaxing the ashes of the previous night's fire back into life, heating up coffee grounds with water that smelt of canvas and horse sweat.

'Almost did a perish,' said Peter, breaking the old man's reverie. 'Two weeks ago. Friggin' truck wouldn't go. Thought I was a goner.'

'Should git yerself a new one,' said Charlie. He spat on the ground, looking straight ahead, the suggestion of a smile on his lips.

Peter looked at him and laughed and the old man laughed with him, presenting his glass. Peter topped it up and took another long swig himself.

*

It was a week since Ruth had told Anne she was no longer welcome at the hotel. Ruth peered through a gap in the curtains, towards the inky blackness of Spencer Gulf. The military authorities had imposed a blackout: no lights within ten miles of the coast were to be visible from sea. Below her, in the front bar, she could hear Harold ushering the last of the drinkers out of the hotel. She reread the opening paragraph of the letter that had arrived that morning from the Chief Protector in Adelaide.

> We have received a complaint about Miss Williams' accommodation and will be obliged if you could furnish this office with more information.

It made her blood boil. So this was her reward for letting Anne Hargreaves into her hotel. She remembered her mother complaining bitterly when Anne's mother had insinuated herself into half a dozen committees within a year of moving to town. And her father's rage at the editorials Mr Hargreaves had run in his newspaper, *The Transcontinental,* at the height of the Great Depression. Attack after attack on the capitalists and their lockouts of mines and saw mills.

There had been something else as well, in the terrible year of 1930, when swagmen and bagmen roamed the countryside and scraps of leather and horse dung had to do for winter fuel. A misunderstanding at a church fete over whether a cake was for sale or merely on display. Had Anne's mother refused to sell it to Ruth's mother? Ruth couldn't remember exactly. But she remembered clearly that the split-second humiliation her mother experienced had calcified into rock-hard anger within a day.

Harold thumped his way up the staircase and into their room. 'Still reading that letter?' he asked.

'Yes. That bloody Anne Hargreaves.'

'Gin-shepherd if ever there was one,' said Harold, standing by the door, his singlet tight against his belly. 'Probably wants Grace for herself.'

'Well, she won't get her,' said Ruth. *And neither will you, Mr Anderson,* she thought, for she'd seen the way he looked at the girl.

*

Peter Dingo heard the church bells ringing out for everyone but him. He woke quickly, feeling rested and strong after a night in a proper bed, away from sun, dogs and wind. He pulled on a pair of trousers, opened the door to the balcony and revelled in the still-cool morning air on his bare chest and arms. A flock of white cockatoos in a red gum across the street guffawed through their early morning calisthenics. Across the inlet, smoke curled from a hundred rough chimneys.

And beyond that, two hundred miles away, his grandfather's land.

Fifty years ago, Robert 'Dingo' Lawton had been granted 160 acres of land – the most an Aboriginal man could receive. His farm had been on the edge of marginal country to the north of Port Lincoln, but he'd grubbed the mallee out, sold it for firewood and lived on kangaroo, goanna, bush plum and acacia seed while he'd slowly stocked his land and sunk wells.

After five years he had a place any man would be proud of, a place to which he could happily take his new white bride. The good people of the colony of South Australia were scandalised. Soon after the marriage, his lease to the land was cancelled.

Peter knew that while he was considered a white man by most in Port Augusta, and was extended all the privileges that went with it, technically he wasn't able to drink or even reside at a hotel without an exemption from the Aborigines Act. He could even be stopped from leaving the state. The breakfast smells of sausages and eggs wafted up from the kitchen and he breathed them in, feeling strong.

*

Ruth entered the relative cool of Taylor's Emporium. Rows of goods and gadgets lined the store. Lanterns, bicycle wheels, mattocks and wicker baskets hung from hooks above the aisles. Taylor also kept the largest selection of women's clothing this side of Adelaide. Plenty of the new Utility fashion, the square 'uniform' shoulders, drab colours, severe lines, nothing with flow or grace. A group of women were chatting and laughing at the counter, Anne among them, her back to Ruth.

Mr Taylor sat behind his desk. A thin man, with dark hair combed neatly to one side and stuck to his head with oil. Anne was holding something up to her body, twirling it as the others looked on.

'Hello, Mrs Anderson,' said one of the women. Anne glanced around and, with a flash of emerald green, the object of their excitement became apparent. Ruth felt sick.

'It's just arrived,' said Anne, a hint of restraint in her voice.

'Beautiful,' murmured Ruth, tight-faced.

'My dress for the concert,' said Anne. 'I couldn't wait to get it home.'

Ruth rummaged through her handbag, muttered an apology – she had left her purse at the hotel – and walked out of the store. Outside, she ignored the postmaster as he dipped his hat. Anger washed over her. Did her family's history in this town count for *nothing?* They were second and third generation people. They had *entitlement,* won from years of hard, bullocking work when the country was new.

*

Peter Dingo breakfasted on fried eggs, bacon, toast and tea, chatting with Grace as she served him. When she smiled, her eyes lit up like church windows. Peter told her he was going to set off for Adelaide soon and would she like ... but then Ruth stormed in and Grace picked up his plate and hurried away to the kitchen.

Back at his truck, Peter grabbed the metal toolbox from the floor of the cab, laid his spanners on the ground and set to work. The roads north of Port Augusta were hell on vehicles. Old Charlie shuffled up with a mug of tea in hand.

'Grab this,' said Peter, pointing to the radiator. Charlie held it as Peter undid the last bolt. They lifted it together and placed it on the ground beside the buckboard.

'When ya goin' back to the bush?' drawled Charlie.

'When I'm good and ready.'

'Ya mean when all ya money's gorn.'

'Yeah.' Peter grabbed a handful of red dirt and rubbed his hands together to knock some of the grease and muck from them. He pulled a tin of Capstan from his back pocket and offered it to Charlie. The old man prised open the tin, took a pinch of the sweet stuff and placed it under his tongue. Peter began rolling a smoke. He'd give the old man a crisp, new five-pound note when he'd finished helping.

'They reckon The Butcher is comin' to town,' said Charlie.

'What! Cleland?'

'Yep.'

'What for?' Peter brushed a bull-ant off his trousers.

'Dunno. Bringin' the Chief Protector with him.'

This was bad news. Peter had seen Professor Cleland, the don from the University of Adelaide, several times while dogging near Ooldea. The Aborigines called him 'The Butcher' on account of his habit of taking a sample of blood from every Aborigine – man, woman or child – he met. He was trying to prove something about them, but he never talked about it.

'I'll keep an eye out,' said Peter, thinking *Jesus, I'll steer clear of those two.*

*

But he couldn't. The next day, at breakfast, sitting at his usual table by the window, Peter noticed the two well-dressed gentlemen enter the dining room. The shorter of the two, a dapper man of fifty or so, bowler in hand, entered first, as if used to getting his own way. Professor Cleland. Behind him came the bespectacled, lanky Chief Protector of Aborigines, Penhall. Ruth, clearly flustered, made them comfortable at a table as far away from the service entrance as possible.

When Peter's meal came he took it in long, thoughtful chews, watching the men. He knew the stories of Cleland. There was a rumour he had asked the doctor at Maitland if he would be prepared to sterilise all the young women at Point Pearce, the government-run station.

Cleland placed a portion of fried egg on a piece of toast, wiping his knife on the crust to remove the soft yolk. The two men talked quietly to each other, keeping an eye on the door to the kitchen.

When the last of the regulars had gone, Grace began to clear away the dishes. Peter gave her a quick smile, conscious of Cleland and Penhall. Grace approached their table.

'May I take your plates?' she asked.

'You may,' said Penhall. She quickly cleared their table. As she turned to go, Cleland put his hand on her arm. 'Wait,' he said. 'You're Grace Williams, aren't you?'

Grace nodded and managed a faint 'Yes'.

'We'd like to have a chat with you,' said Penhall, looking over the rim of his glasses at her.

'And with Mrs Anderson,' said Cleland, patting her arm. 'Go and get her for us please.'

Seconds later, Ruth hurried into the room, followed by Grace. Peter remained at his table, half a cup of lukewarm coffee in front of him. He got the newspaper from the sideboard and pretended to read it, following the conversation as it hit upon Grace's circumstances, the death of her mother, her living arrangements, and the anonymous complaint. Ruth offered information as it was required. Grace said very little.

'You know,' said Cleland, adjusting his collar, 'we could always send you to Point Pearce if things don't work out well.'

Peter's chair scraped the floorboards as he rose. 'I think you'll find that Miss Williams turns twenty-one in a few months' time,' he said, facing the two men.

'Who are you?' asked Cleland, looking him over.

'And there's very little you can do once that happens,' said Peter. 'Under the Act, your guardianship expires at twenty-one.'

'Who *are* you, sir?' snapped Cleland, his face reddening as he stood and tossed his napkin onto the table.

'Peter,' he said. 'Peter Dingo. Grandson of Robert Lawton.'

Cleland nodded quickly, looking as if he'd bitten on a lemon. 'Ah yes,' he said. 'Your people over-reached themselves, didn't they?'

Peter caught a quick glance from Grace that softened him and he smiled wryly. 'Your people took everything we had, even the little things you gave us. We haven't over-reached ourselves. Not yet.' He turned and walked out of the room.

*

Before they left for the interior, Penhall and Cleland paid Ruth Anderson another visit. As a result of their enquiries, they told her, they had concluded that a hotel was not the proper place for a part-Aboriginal girl. As Ruth stared out the dining-room window and thought of how impossible life would be without Grace, she heard Cleland mutter about the pernicious effect an octoroon like Peter Dingo could have on Grace's development. They were investigating an alternative placement and would speak further on the matter when they returned from their survey of ration stations in the north, in a week's time.

'To whom will she go?' asked Ruth, but neither man responded. She already knew.

Later, in the front bar of the Royal Mail, Harold Anderson was getting into the swing of it. The presence of Cleland and the Protector had set him off. 'We should just fence off Spear Creek,' he said, grimacing. 'Round up all the black bastards and leave 'em there. No missionaries or government men trying to tell us what we can or can't do with them.'

Charlie shook his head and muttered to himself. Peter Dingo stood alongside him, at the edge of the bar. Through the window above the bar the sky was bleeding out. A couple of men uttered a 'Too right' or 'Yeah'.

'This town'd be bloody lost without 'em,' said Peter Dingo, and the bar fell silent. Constable Johnston turned to Peter and nodded to him in quiet agreement.

'You're joking,' said Harold. He had two inches and sixty-odd pounds on Peter, but the lean dogger had an assuredness of movement and a loose-limbed way of holding himself that gave him a presence beyond his stature. There were stories that suggested he could fight, but no one in town was anxious to find out if they were true or not.

Peter shrugged and took a sip of beer. 'Stations round here would grind to a halt. It's the blackfellas do most of the mustering.'

'Well, we could let some of 'em out to work now and then,' said Harold, wiping a glass.

'Yeah, the good ones,' piped up a railway worker.

'And lock 'em back up at Spear Creek when it's holiday time? When the stations have no more use for 'em?' asked Peter. The tone of his voice had hardly changed, and the lines around his eyes could have been mistaken for the makings of a smile.

'Yeah,' said Harold, his mouth tightening, conscious of a roomful of men weighing each word he uttered for hesitation and retreat. The room stilled.

Peter lowered his glass to the bar. He turned and walked to the front door and then out and into the gathering dark.

*

After closing time, Ruth stood in front of her mirror, the emerald dress exotic and rich against her skin. She heard Harold approaching from the hallway, floorboards creaking under his weight.

'This what you've been talking about?' he asked.

'Yes,' she said. 'This is the dress. Ruined.'

Harold opened his mouth, then shut it again. Ruth watched him in the mirror. He moved towards her. Through a slit in the heavy velvet curtains the mudflats spread below them like a stain on a sheet. 'Come here Mrs Anderson,' he said. 'I'll tell you if it's ruined or not.' He stood behind her, one arm around her waist, the other rucking the silk over her skin, the whiff of mudflat suddenly strong.

Ruth twisted away.

III

The first light of day slanted across the town, placing a tiny shadow beside each stone in the hotel yard. Charlie had already been up an hour. He sat on the back step, a cigarette rolled and stashed behind his ear for later. Grace came out of the washhouse in her hibiscus dress, carrying a basket of linen. He rose to help her.

'It's okay, Charlie,' she said.

He watched her as she worked. She took care not to let the ends of the sheets drag in the dirt, swinging them up and over the line in one graceful, strong movement. She was the finest-looking girl in town. Dark, thick hair, long strong limbs the colour of honey. He wondered about his own girl, Rosie, and her full-blood mother at Granite Downs Station. At least they were given rations there.

'Concert tonight,' he said.

'Yeah.' Grace threw another sheet over the line.

Charlie heard footsteps behind him in the hallway, coming closer. Ruth walked past him, blinking as she emerged from the dark of the hotel into the yard whirling brightly with sheets.

'When you've done the laundry I'd like you to give the dining room a bit of a dust,' she said to Grace.

'Yes, ma'am,' said Grace, jamming a peg onto a sheet.

After Ruth had gone, Charlie cleared his throat and spat in the dirt beside the step. 'Don't let her get you down, missy,' he said. 'Some people just don't know how to say please.'

'Some people don't have to,' said Grace.

Charlie laughed. 'True enough,' he said, wincing as he raised himself off the step. One of these days, he knew, the knee would go and then he'd be stuffed. No good to anybody. Grace hung the last of the sheets, picked up her basket and headed to the washhouse for the next load. 'You got yerself a dress for the concert?' he called.

'Aww, Charlie. You know I can't go.'

'You should,' he said, knowing it was impossible. There would be no dark-skinned people at the concert, just as none were allowed into the picture show in town on a Sunday afternoon, and only in the front stalls on Friday and Saturday nights.

*

When breakfast was done, Grace took morning tea inside her room. There was a knock on the door. Grace opened it. Ruth.

'Mrs Anderson,' she said. 'What's wrong?'

'Nothing, my dear,' said Ruth. 'But I have a favour to ask. May I come in?'

'Of course,' said Grace, moving aside. She nearly motioned for Ruth to sit on the one chair her tiny room allowed, but stopped, unsure what to do. She couldn't remember having Ruth in her room before.

'I want you to accompany me to the concert tonight,' said Ruth.

'What!?'

Ruth repeated herself.

'But how ... I mean, I don't have a dress,' said Grace, panic rising in her throat.

'That's okay. I have just the thing,' said Ruth.

'But—'

'You can knock off today at five. Then come up to my room and I'll dress you.'

*

Later, Charlie stopped Ruth as she was going upstairs. 'The girl tells me you're taking her to the concert,' he said.

'That's right, Charlie.'

'You got her a dress?' asked Charlie. 'I thought maybe I could help. Pitch in, y'know.'

Ruth nodded. 'Sure, Charlie. What have you got?'

'Here,' said the old man, reaching into his pocket. He drew out the five-pound note Peter Dingo had given him for helping fix the buckboard. Ruth tucked it into the bosom of her dress and left him at the foot of the stairs.

*

Grace wished she was anywhere else as she stood in Ruth's room. Ruth laid the dress on her bed. Emerald green silk, the sort of rich colour reserved for parrots, and then used only sparingly by them. Grace turned to Ruth in protest. It was far too beautiful. 'Nonsense,' replied Ruth and told the girl that she had owned the dress for ages and never worn it. It wasn't her colour. But Grace, with her skin, would look wonderful in it. All Grace could do was shake her head. She stood there, trembling, while Ruth dressed her.

*

At dusk, Charlie sauntered through the yard and found Peter Dingo parking his truck at the back of the hotel.

'What are you so happy about, old man?' Peter asked him. 'Going to the concert?'

'Not for the world,' Charlie grinned. 'But, oh Lord, my dress is going.'

Peter climbed out of the cab. 'Whatdaya mean?'

'Bought the girlie a dress,' said the old man, his voice low but proud. 'Grace. She's wearing it. But don't tell her,' he added. 'Don't tell her it was me.' He put a tobacco-stained finger to his lips.

'Where'd you get a dress from?'

Charlie caught a trace of jealousy in Peter's voice and grinned again. 'From the missus,' he said. 'The five quid you gave me.'

'From Ruth?' said Peter. 'Why would she do that?' he said, more to himself than Charlie, and pondered the question as he made his way upstairs. *Why would Grace even be going to the concert?* He scrambled into his best clothes and hurried back down.

*

As Peter was getting dressed, Ruth and Grace were walking towards the church. Grace, bewildered, allowed her employer to hold her arm as they walked down the street. Ruth silently marked off the properties her parents had owned when her family meant everything to this town. *The Commercial Hotel was ours,* she thought. *And that three-bedroom stone cottage next to it. This block of land across from it, and that one further down the road.* As a ten-year-old, walking up and down this dusty street, the tang of ownership had been as strong and sweet as a stolen orange. *She won't have her,* she thought. *She won't.*

In the distance, beyond the town, the Flinders Range was merging with the evening sky. A straggle of Aboriginal children at a low section of the churchyard wall were taking turns to hoist each other up for a glimpse of the concert. Ruth and Grace walked past them and into the churchyard, towards the welcoming committee. Beyond them, nearer the stage, post office girls mingled with flat-footed clerks, waiting for the dancing to begin.

Ruth picked out Anne Hargreaves among the committee, laughing as she chatted with a smartly uniformed man, her dress shimmering in the evening light. Miss Shadforth, the missionary, noticed Ruth and Grace approaching. 'Oh Lord!' she said, taking a step back.

As she saw what she was being led to, Grace tried to snatch her arm away from Ruth. The older woman tightened her grip and marched her up to Anne's little bevy. Port Augusta's finest.

'Good evening ladies. Don't we all look wonderful tonight?' said Ruth.

Several women gasped and Anne broke off her conversation and turned. Her breath left her. She couldn't speak. She stared at the Aboriginal maid wearing her dress. *Her* beautiful dress. Grace's face burned and she looked down at the ground.

Then Anne stepped closer. A nerve under her eye twitched and a sudden deep breath straightened her and Ruth waited for her to slap Grace, to make it complete. But, before she could, the missionary woman thrust out an arm, grabbed Anne by the elbow and pulled her away, towards the church.

Grace felt the eyes of every white woman in town on her. She wrenched her arm free and ran down the path, through the churchyard entrance, and onto the street.

Peter watched her go, then turned back to see Ruth walking up to the major, a smile on her face. *Bugger this town,* he thought. By tomorrow afternoon he'd be in Adelaide. Maybe he'd give Sydney another go.

Through the vacant lot he went and into the yard of the hotel. Golden light leaked from the doorway of Grace's room. He stood outside it, hesitated, knocked and said, 'It's me, Peter.' She opened the door and stood there in the warm glow of the hurricane lamp, her hair thick and clean and ponytailed against the honeyed skin of her neck, her eyes reddened. Behind her, on the bed, lay an open, battered suitcase.

She looked straight at him, proud but scared. Something moved inside him – something big.

'You're leaving, aren't you?' he said.

Grace nodded and Peter was close enough now to smell the lemony scent of laundry soap on skin. 'I could take you to Sydney with me,' he said, the words escaping before he knew he would say them.

'Adelaide will do,' said Grace.

Peter nodded. 'Yeah. It will.' He remembered the name of the street he'd been entrusted with. Snatches of double bass and laughter carried to them on the breeze.

'I'll knock,' he said. 'First light.'

*

Early the next morning, Charlie shuffled towards the counter of the post office. He was carrying a soft parcel, wrapped in brown paper, tied with string. 'Can ya help me with this?' he asked the postmaster.

'Sure thing, Charlie. Who's it for?'

'Rosie Farquhar. Care of Granite Downs Station.'

The postmaster wrote the name carefully on the parcel.

'My daughter,' Charlie smiled.

Acknowledgements

Thanks to all those who have read and commented on these stories but especially Bruce McClintock, Tania Madigan, Wallace McKitrick, Sarah Gordon-Smith, Jenny Toune, Tim Taylor, Timo Bishop, Robbie Brechin, John McBeath, Beth McLean, Rose Ward and Anne Rothfusz Johnson.

Thanks to Robin Green for the illustrations. Love your work, Rob.

Thanks to Big Nan for giving me the story of the dress, to everyone at Wakefield Press, especially Ryan Paine, and to Arts SA for allowing me funds to write.

None of this would have been possible without Tania's patience, support and love.

Some of the stories have been published or awarded prizes elsewhere. 'The Colour of Kerosene' won the Josephine Ulrick Literary Prize in 2008 and was published in *The Griffith Review,* no.22 (2008); 'Sunlight' in *The Griffith Review,* no.23 (2009); 'Semaphore' in *Wet Ink,* no.8 (2007);

and 'You Matter to God' in *Sleepers Almanac,* no.6 (2010). 'The Smell of Touch' was shortlisted for the Fish International Short Story Prize in 2010.

This collection was shortlisted for the 2009 Adelaide Festival Awards for Literature.

Back Cover Material

In these fourteen stories, Cameron Raynes traverses landscapes of regret, joy and redemption. In a country town, a woman plots to ruin her rival with an act steeped in racism. A welfare worker is asked to spy on a colleague. And in the award-winning title story, a taxi driver accepts a fare he knows he shouldn'

They headed east, the nude hills of the Geraldton plains, stripped of their trees a century before, leaning into them on both sides as the car climbed into the marginal country. Behind him, Luke heard the gurgle of fluid sluicing out of a bladder and into a cup, smelt the sweet stink of cheap wine. It occurred to him that it was not too late to turn back.

'Reading the stories in *Kerosene* will put dirt under your fingernails. Raynes's vision is hard-edged and sometimes downright brutal yet it's studded with empathy, compassion and truth.'

Patrick Allington

BIN TRAVELER FORM

Cut By: PEDRO CASTILLO #15 **Qty** 26 **Date** 07-14-26

Scanned By: _____ **Qty** _____ **Date** _____

Scanned Batch ID's _____

Notes / Exceptions

_____